✴RICHARD PAUL EVANS✴

A STEP OF

Faith

THE FOURTH JOURNAL OF *THE WALK* SERIES

SIMON & SCHUSTER PAPERBACKS

NEW YORK LONDON TORONTO SYDNEY NEW DELHI

Simon & Schuster Paperbacks
A Division of Simon & Schuster, Inc.
1230 Avenue of the Americas
New York, NY 10020

First Simon & Schuster trade paperback edition April 2014

SIMON & SCHUSTER PAPERBACKS and colophon are registered
trademarks of Simon & Schuster, Inc.

For information about special discounts for bulk purchases,
please contact Simon & Schuster Special Sales at
1-866-506-1949 or business@simonandschuster.com.

The Simon & Schuster Speakers Bureau can bring authors
to your live event. For more information or to book an event,
contact the Simon & Schuster Speakers Bureau at
1-866-248-3049 or visit our website at www.simonspeakers.com.

Designed by Davina Mock-Maniscalco

Manufactured in the United States of America

5   7   9   10   8   6   4

Library of Congress Cataloging-in-Publication Data is available.

ISBN 978-1-4516-2829-6
ISBN 978-1-4516-2830-2 (pbk)
ISBN 978-1-4516-2834-0 (ebook)

✦ ACKNOWLEDGMENTS ✦

would like to thank the following for their assistance: Once again, my writing assistant, travel companion and daughter, Jenna Evans Welch. (And Ally, who came along for the ride. And Sam, who also came, but against his will.) My friends at Simon & Schuster: Jonathan Karp, Carolyn Reidy, my editor Trish Todd (and Molly Lindley) and copy editor Gypsy da Silva. Mike and Cathy Hankins of the Southern Hotel in Ste. Genevieve, Kelly Glad, Judge Samuel D. McVey, Dr. Steve Schlozman, and The Cancer Learning Center at Huntsman Cancer Institute at the University of Utah.

My staff: Diane Glad, Heather McVey, Barry Evans, Karen Christoffersen, Doug Osmond (Osmonds rock!), Lisa Johnson, and Camille Shosted. And my agent, Laurie Liss. Good work. I'll most likely kill you in the morning. (Just seeing if you really read my books.)

*To my daughters, Jenna Lyn and Allyson-Danica.
The Okefenokee wouldn't have been
the same without you.
I love you, girls. *

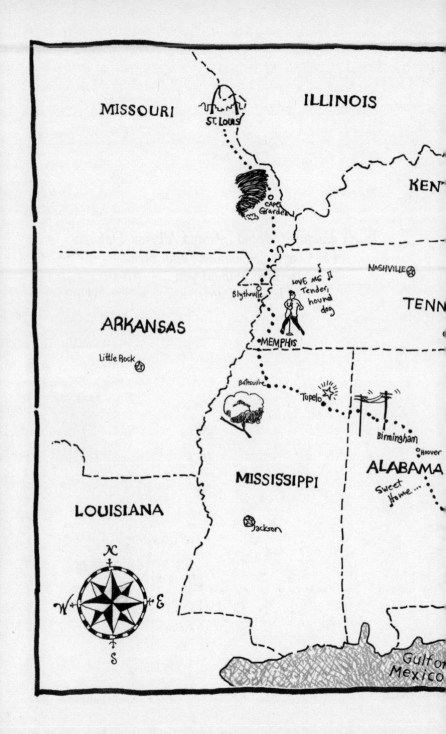

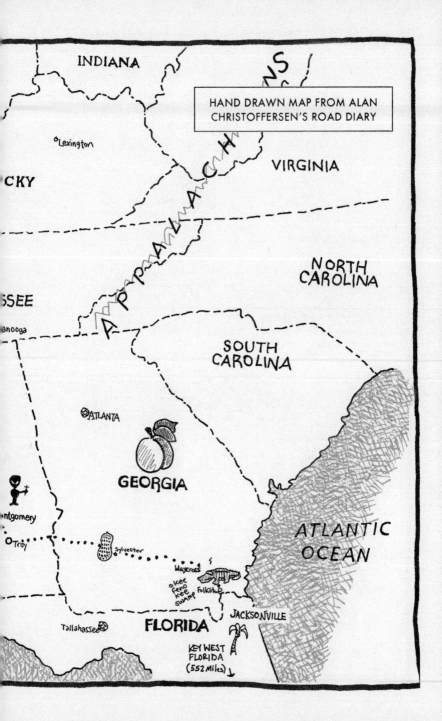

HAND DRAWN MAP FROM ALAN
CHRISTOFFERSEN'S ROAD DIARY

INDIANA

VIRGINIA

°Lexington

CKY

APPALACHIANS

NORTH
CAROLINA

SSEE

anooga

SOUTH
CAROLINA

°ATLANTA

GEORGIA

ntgomery

Troy

Sylvester

Waycross

o·kee·
Feno·
kee·
swamp Folkston

ATLANTIC
OCEAN

Tallahassee

FLORIDA

JACKSONVILLE

KEY WEST
FLORIDA
(552 Miles) ↓

Faith is the strength by which a shattered world
shall emerge into the light.

—Helen Keller

A STEP OF

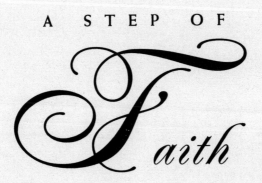

More than once, usually after getting a strange glance from an occupant of a passing car, I've wondered what people think of me—a lone man, unshaven, long hair spilling from beneath his hat, walking alone along some forsaken stretch of highway. They wouldn't likely guess that I once owned a prestigious advertising agency, or a multimillion-dollar home, or shared a love that others only dream about. Nor would they guess how badly my heart's been broken. We don't think those things about strangers.

The truth is, they probably don't think about me at all. Or at least not for very long. We have become proficient at blocking each other out. Just like we block advertising noise. I'm not claiming this is a sign of societal decay or moral deficiency. I think it's a necessity. There are far too many people for us to think about each of them during our short stay on earth—like the thousands of books in a library we haven't time to read in an afternoon. But this is no excuse to cease browsing. For every now and then, we find that one book that reaches us deep inside and introduces us to ourselves. And, in someone else's story, we come to understand our own.

✳

I don't know how you found me, but my name is Alan Christoffersen. And this is the story of my walk.

PROLOGUE

Maybe, if we just accepted our deaths,
we might finally start to live.

Alan Christoffersen's diary

Am I dying?

It's a stupid question, really, as we've all got an expiration date. I guess the real question is not *if*, but *when*.

As I was walking through the South Dakota Badlands—before I knew something was wrong with me—I had this thought: *What if we all carried little timers that counted down the days of our lives?* Maybe the timer's a bit dramatic. Just the date would do. It could be tattooed on our foreheads like the expiration date on a milk bottle.

It might be a good thing. Maybe we'd stop wasting our lives worrying about things that never happen, or collecting things that we can't take with us. We'd probably treat people better. We certainly wouldn't be screaming at someone who had a day left. Maybe people would finally stop living like they're immortal. Maybe we would finally learn how to live.

I've wondered if, perhaps, at some deep, subconscious level, we really do know our time. I've heard stories of people spontaneously buying life insurance or writing wills just days before an unforeseen calamity takes their lives.

In my own life I've seen evidence of this. My mother—

who died when I was eight—told my father more than once that she didn't think she would live to an old age or, to her great sadness, to see her grandchildren. Some might say that she jinxed herself, but I don't think so. My mother wasn't a pessimist. I think she knew.

Whether we know our time or not, it doesn't change the truth—there is a clock ticking for all of us. I suppose this weighs heavily on my mind right now because my clock seems to be ticking a little more loudly lately. A brain tumor will do that to you.

✦

If you're picking up my story for the first time, my name is Alan Christoffersen and I'm walking across America. I started 258 days ago from my home (or what *was* my home) in Seattle, Washington. I'm walking 3,500 miles to Key West, Florida.

A day ago I was found unconscious on the side of Highway 61, about forty-five miles from where I am now—the St. Louis University Hospital. All I know for certain about my condition is that the doctors found a brain tumor. This came to me as a complete surprise.

Almost as surprising as my wife's death—which is why I'm walking to begin with.

Nearly ten months ago my wife, McKale, was paralyzed in a horse-riding accident. While I cared for her, my advertising agency's clients were stolen by my partner, Kyle Craig, and the loss of income coupled with mounting medical bills sent me spiraling into bankruptcy. My cars were repossessed and my home was foreclosed on. A month later, when McKale died of complications, I lost everything.

At the time, I wanted to take my life. Instead, I decided to take a walk—one that would take me as far away from Seattle as physically possible. I'm a little more than halfway. Perhaps death has been following me all along.

CHAPTER

One

The strength of a friendship can be
measured by the weight of the burden
it's willing to share. (If you want to test
this just ask someone to help you move.)

Alan Christoffersen's diary

Where was I? My stomach ached. My head spun. Then re-
membrance returned. *St. Louis. I'm in a hospital in St. Louis.
McKale is gone. Still gone. Always gone.*

My room was dark and still except for the soft hum-
ming and occasional beeps from the monitors next to
my bed. I was awake for nearly a minute before I realized that I wasn't alone. My friend Falene was sitting
quietly next to me. My anxiety softened at the sight
of her.

"Hi," I said. My mouth was dry.

"Hi," she echoed softly. "How are you feeling?"

"Fantastic."

She smiled sadly. "Are you still dizzy?"

"A little." I shut my eyes as a wave of nausea passed
through me. When I could speak, I opened my eyes.
"What time is it?"

"It's a little past nine."

"Oh," I said, as if it meant something. ". . . Day or
night?"

"Day. I kept the blinds down so you could sleep."

"How long have you been here?"

"I've been here all night. With your father."

I slowly looked around the small, dim room. "My father?"

"I made him get something to eat. He hadn't left your side since yesterday. I don't think he's eaten since he got here."

"That's not good."

"No, it isn't." She reached over and took my hand. "He didn't want to leave your side. People love you, you know."

"I know," I said softly. I squeezed her hand as I looked into her eyes. I could see the fear in them behind her tears. She was so beautiful. And she was so good to me. *Why was she so good to me?* I hated seeing her so afraid. "Everything is going to be okay."

She leaned forward and raised my hand to her cheek. A tear fell on my hand. Then another. After a moment she leaned back and wiped her eyes. "You'd better be okay."

"I will be," I said. "I'll be fine."

It was a hollow assertion. We both knew that I had no idea whether or not I would be.

The room fell into silence. After a moment she said, "I never got back to you with Kyle's number."

Several weeks earlier I had asked her to find my former business partner Kyle Craig's phone number for me. With all that had happened since then, I'd forgotten about it. "Did you find him?"

"Sort of . . ." she said, her expression turning dark. "Remember I told you that there were a lot of people looking for him?"

"Yes. Is he in trouble?"

"He's dead."

Her words stunned me. "Dead?"

She nodded.

"Someone killed him?"

"He committed suicide."

I didn't speak for nearly a minute, my mind processing this new reality. "When did it happen?"

"About a month ago."

I closed my eyes. I had tried to call Kyle to tell him that I forgave him for what he had done. I now realized that even though I hadn't had the chance to say it to him, I truly had forgiven him, because the strongest emotion I felt at the news of his death wasn't the need for revenge or even anger, but sorrow. Not for me, but for Kyle. Sorrow for the choices he'd made that led him to where he'd ended up.

I slowly breathed out. "Oh, Kyle."

My mind skipped back to when I'd brought him on at my newborn agency. Those were adventurous days, and even though we worked too much, there were good times and lots of laughter. To celebrate our first million-dollar client we bought a dozen laser-tag guns from the Sharper Image catalogue and played laser tag in our office after work. McKale thought we were crazy. I remember her rolling her eyes and saying, "Boys and their toys." We just thought we were unstoppable. Our sky had no limit. Kyle had not only shared my dreams, but helped fuel them. He helped me dream them. *Those were the best of days.* I was sincerely sorry that Kyle was gone.

"He didn't deserve that," I said softly.

Falene narrowed her eyes. "You're a better person than I am," she said, "because I thought he got exactly what he deserved."

"What he did to me was wrong, but he could have changed. He could have been the man he once was."

"You amaze me," Falene said. "After all that he did to you, you still forgive him?"

I turned and looked at her. "I suppose I have."

✦

It was another ten minutes before my father walked into the room. He was wearing the same clothes he'd had on the day before. When I was younger this would have embarrassed me.

"Hi, son," he said. His eyes were dark, ringed with exhaustion. More disturbing to me was his expression—the same stoic, gray mask he wore the week my mother was dying. I hated seeing it on his face again, though not as much for my sake as his. He walked up to the side of my bed. "How are you feeling?"

"Fine," I said. It was a fib—the kind of reply you give when you don't want to give one. I was glad he didn't press me on it.

"I just checked at the nurses' station. The doctor will be here around noon with your test results."

"I feel like I'm waiting for the jury's verdict," I said. I looked back at Falene. "How are you doing?"

"I'm okay," she said.

"How's your brother?"

She frowned. "I still don't know where he is. He's disappeared."

"I'm sorry," I said. I didn't want to cause her more distress so I let it go. "Think I could get something to eat?"

"I'll let the nurse know that you're awake," Falene said. She stood and walked out of the room.

I turned to my dad. "Falene said you haven't been eating."

"I haven't been hungry."

"You still need to eat," I said.

"You worry about yourself."

Just then there was a short knock and someone else entered my room. At first I thought it was a nurse. It wasn't. It was Nicole, the woman I had stayed with in Spokane after being mugged. When she saw me, her eyes welled up with tears. "Alan." She walked quickly to me and we embraced. "I got here as soon as I could."

"How did you know I was here?"

"I told her," my father said.

My father, an accountant, had taken on Nicole's finances after she had inherited money from her landlord.

Nicole kissed my cheek, then leaned back, looking into my eyes. "How are you feeling?"

"I'm okay."

"I can tell you're lying," she said. "This feels like déjà vu, doesn't it? You're spending way too much time in hospitals."

"I feel like I'm just walking from one hospital to the next," I said. "Hopefully there's a good one in Key West."

"Hopefully you'll never find out," she replied. She kissed my cheek again, then stood, looking at my father. "Hello, Mr. Christoffersen. It's good to see you again."

He reached out his hand. "It's good to see you again too."

"Your dad has been such an angel," Nicole said. "I'd be lost without him."

My father looked very pleased. "It's nothing," he said. "I wish all my clients were so pleasant."

Nicole smiled, then turned back to me. "It's just so good to see you." She leaned over and hugged me again. When we parted, I noticed that Falene had slipped back into the room. Her eyes were darting back and forth between Nicole and me.

"They'll be here with your breakfast in a few minutes," Falene said.

"Thank you," I said. "Nicole, you remember my friend, Falene."

Nicole looked at Falene. "Of course," she said. "You came to my house in Spokane."

"That's right," Falene said softly.

Nicole quickly turned back to me. "So what happened? What are you doing here?"

"I started getting dizzy a few weeks ago. On the way to St. Louis I passed out on the side of the road. I woke up here."

"Thank goodness someone stopped to help you," she said. "So they don't know what's going on?"

"He has a brain tumor," Falene said, sounding slightly annoyed.

Nicole looked at her. "I know," she said. "That's why I'm here."

"The doctor will be in around noon to give us an update," my father said.

Nicole took my hand. "Then I got here just in time."

The room fell into silence. Falene looked at Nicole for a moment, then said, "I'm going to get some rest."

"Of course," I said.

"I'll watch over him," Nicole said.

Falene glanced furtively at her, then said, "I'll be back before noon." She turned and walked out of the room.

I watched her go, feeling uncomfortable about the tension between the two women. The room again fell into silence. After a moment I asked Nicole, "How is Kailamai doing?"

"She's doing really well. I couldn't ask for a better roommate. You were definitely inspired to match us up."

"Did your sister ever come to visit?" Nicole looked as if she didn't understand my question so I continued. ". . . You were going to get together for a vacation at Bullman Beach."

"I can't believe you remembered that," she said. "Yes, she came in May. We had a great time. It was . . . healing." She took a deep breath. "So, back to you. Was this a complete surprise?"

"A gradual surprise," I said. "I got dizzy partway through South Dakota and ended up in a hospital in Mitchell. But the doctor there thought it was just vertigo and gave me some pills. It didn't hit me hard again until just before St. Louis."

"We're lucky it was someplace you could be found," my father said. "Instead of some country back road."

"You do know that you've walked more than halfway," Nicole said. "I looked it up on MapQuest. Your halfway mark was a town in Iowa called Sydney. You probably don't even remember walking through the town, do you?"

I thought about Analise and the night I had spent at her house. "Yes, I remember," I said simply.

Just then a nurse walked in carrying a tray. "Breakfast, Mr. Christoffersen."

Nicole stepped back as the nurse prepped the meal,

setting it on the table over my bed. Almost everything on the tray was mostly water. Jell-O. Juice. Melon. I took a few bites.

After the nurse left, I said to Nicole, "Think you could find me some real food?"

CHAPTER

Two

"Wait and see" is no easier now
than it was as a child.

Alan Christoffersen's diary

Falene returned to my room about ten minutes before noon. She looked more tired than when she had left and still looked upset.

"Did you sleep?" I asked.

She shook her head. "Not really. The only place I could find was the waiting room. There were a lot of screaming kids."

"You should have just rested in here," I said. "Like my father."

I pointed my thumb at my father, who was reclined in a chair, his head back, and mouth wide open as he snored.

"That's okay," Falene said. "I don't think I could have slept anyway."

My doctor arrived a few minutes after noon, studying an iPad as he walked in. He glanced up at all of us and said, "Good morning. Or afternoon. Whichever it is." He looked at me. "I'm Dr. Kelson. How are you feeling?"

"Tired."

"Still dizzy?"

"A little."

My dad woke, wiping his eyes and yawning loudly before realizing where he was. "Sorry," he said.

"Welcome back," Nicole said.

"Did I miss anything?"

"No," she said. "The doctor just got here."

"I'm Dr. Kelson," the doctor said to my father. He turned back to me. "Are we free to speak, or should I send everyone out?"

I didn't like the question or the way he asked it. It sounded foreboding. "I'd like them to be here," I said. "For the verdict."

He nodded. "All right then." He raised his voice a little. "You already know that we found a tumor. The question is what *kind*. After another review of your MRI and CT scans and after consulting with a few of my colleagues, we feel confident that the abnormality detected is a meningioma." He paused as if the word might mean something to me. It didn't, but it sounded bad.

My father's brow fell. "What's that?"

"A meningioma is a tumor of the membrane that surrounds the brain and spinal cord."

Falene lifted her hand to her forehead.

"I know it sounds bad," the doctor said. "But it could be much worse. Most meningiomas are operable and benign. Not all, but most."

"How do you know if it's benign?" my father asked.

"That will require a biopsy. Meningiomas are generally slow-growing, so sometimes we take a wait-and-see approach, but since you're already experiencing symptoms, it's likely that the tumor is putting pressure on your brain. I recommend that we perform surgery to remove the tumor and relieve the pressure. Then, after the surgery, we'll do a biopsy and determine whether the tumor is benign or malignant."

"If it's benign?" my father asked.

"Then there's no need for further treatment and we send you on your way."

My father nodded. "And if it's malignant?"

"Then we'll determine whether or not the cancer has spread to other parts of the body and go after it with all the arrows in our quiver."

"Which means I won't be able to walk," I said.

The doctor turned back toward me. "No, you should be able to walk."

"He means cross-country," Falene said. "He's walking across America. He's already halfway."

The doctor looked at Falene for a moment as if he was trying to decide whether or not she was being serious, then turned back to me. "No, you would have to postpone that. So Missouri isn't your home?"

"No," I said.

He nodded thoughtfully. "You'll probably want to be treated closer to home. It wouldn't make sense traveling this far for care."

"If I had a home," I said.

"You can come back with me," Nicole said. "I've quit my job, so I could take care of you full-time." She looked at me fondly. "It will be like old times."

I noticed the look on Falene's face.

"It's your decision," my father said. "But I think you should come back to Pasadena with me. I'd like to have you close, and we're just four miles from the UCLA medical center." Then he added, "It would be a good place to start rebuilding your life."

I looked at him, wondering what he had meant by his latter comment.

"UCLA is a top-ranked cancer hospital," the doctor

said. "In fact, a former colleague of mine is out there. He's one of the top neurosurgeons in the country. I'd be happy to contact him."

"We'd appreciate that," my father said.

"I could still come down to help," Nicole said.

"We could write it off," my father said, always in accountant mode.

"What if I do nothing?" I asked.

Falene glared at me.

Peculiarly, the doctor looked less surprised by my question than everyone else in the room. "If you weren't already showing symptoms, maybe nothing. At least for a while. But even if it's benign, a brain tumor can still cause significant problems. In the short term, you'll only get sicker. In the long term, it could cause disability or take your life. Of course it's up to you, but I don't see that doing nothing's a real option."

Falene was still glaring at me.

"Any more questions?" the doctor asked.

"When can I leave?" I asked.

"You should spend the night," he said. "You can leave in the morning."

"I'll have to book our flight anyway," my father said.

"With your permission I'll contact the cancer center at UCLA and make a referral," the doctor said.

"You have our permission," my father said.

The doctor looked at me for confirmation. "Is that all right with you?"

"Yes."

"Okay. I'll tell the nurses to prepare for your discharge in the morning."

"Thanks, Doc," my father said.

"Don't mention it," he replied. He walked out of the room.

"That's good news, right?" Nicole said. "Meningioma?"

"Considering what it could have been, I think you might have just dodged a bullet," my father said. He put his hand on my arm. "It will be nice having you around for a while. Just like old times." He looked at me for a moment, then said, slightly smiling, "Hopefully better."

I nodded.

"So you'll be leaving in the morning," Nicole said. "I'll book my flight for tomorrow afternoon. That way I can spend the night." Nicole turned to Falene. "I can spell you."

"I'm okay," Falene said.

"You look exhausted," my father said bluntly.

"I'm okay," Falene repeated. She looked at me. "What do you want me to do?"

She looked exhausted, but I could tell that she was bothered by Nicole's intrusion. "Whatever you want."

For what felt like a long time she looked at me with an expression I didn't understand. Then she walked up and kissed me on the forehead. "Okay. Get some rest." She walked out of the room and I watched her go, sensing that something terrible had just happened. I wanted to call her back. I almost did, but Nicole broke my train of thought.

"When would you like me to come to Pasadena?"

CHAPTER

Three

I'm going home. Wherever
that is these days.

Alan Christoffersen's diary

I woke the next morning just a little after sunrise, the first rays of dawn stealing through the blinds, striping the wall across from my bed with amber, horizontal bars. Nicole was sitting next to me. Her blond hair was slightly matted to one side and she was looking at me. "Morning, handsome," she said softly.

I rubbed a hand over my eyes. "Good morning."

"You slept well."

"You've been here the whole night?"

"Every minute of it," she said. "But I wasn't awake the whole night. I fell asleep around one, so I got some rest."

"You didn't need to do that," I said.

"I know. I wanted to."

"Thank you." I looked around the room. "Where's my father?"

"He went back to his hotel. He said he'd check out, then come over here to get you. He'll be here before nine."

"Where's Falene?"

"I don't know. I haven't seen her since she left yesterday afternoon." She brushed a long strand of hair back from her face. "How are you feeling?"

"A little better than yesterday."

"That's encouraging," she said.

It wasn't, of course. The tumor wasn't going away until it was cut out of me.

Nicole reached over the bedrail and lifted the St. Christopher that lay on my chest. "You're still wearing the medallion I gave you."

"I never took it off."

She smiled as she ran her thumb over the token. She looked into my eyes. "Do you ever think about the time we spent together?"

"Of course."

"What do you think about it?"

"That depends on if I'm thinking about Angel or Nicole."

"Angel," she said softly. "I almost forgot about her."

"That's a good thing," I said.

She kissed me on the cheek. "That is a good thing. You saved my life."

"I don't—"

She put a finger on my lips. "You did. I'll never be able to repay you for what you did. And I'll never forget the time we spent together. It was the most loving and beautiful experience of my life." Her eyes began welling up with tears. "And here you are again. If something had happened to you . . ." She pulled down the railing, then laid her head on my chest, her eyes meeting mine. "You have to be okay."

I put my hand on her head, my fingers plying through her silky blond hair. "I'm going to be okay. You don't have to worry."

After a moment she raised her head. "Do you remember what you said to me the last time we spoke on the phone?"

I shook my head.

"You promised that I'd see you again. And here we are."

"I hadn't expected it to be quite this soon," I said.

"I'm not complaining." After a moment of silence she said, "The nurse said the doctor would be coming by to see you again before you leave."

"When is that?"

"Your flight's booked for a little after noon. I told them we'd be leaving around ten. Are you glad to be going back with your dad?"

"It will be interesting. It's been more than a decade since I lived at home." I took a deep breath. "I don't know what he's expecting. He made that comment yesterday about rebuilding my life. I wonder if he means now."

"He's just excited to have you home. Why wouldn't he be?" She glanced up at the room's clock. "Would you like me to ask the nurse to bring your breakfast?"

"I'd rather have another catheter put in."

She grinned. "Can I get you something from the cafeteria?"

"Sure. How about waffles or pancakes. Whichever you think looks better. And a side of scrambled eggs."

"Scrambled it is. Anything to drink?"

"Cranberry juice if they have it."

"Pancakes, scrambled eggs, and cranberry juice."

I raked my hair back with my hand. "I'll get dressed while you're gone."

She stood. "I'll hurry."

I watched her as she walked out of the room. I knew she had feelings for me. I just didn't know what to do with them. Nicole was beautiful and sweet and I knew her almost as intimately as I had ever known anyone. I guess that happens when you walk with someone to the edge of their life.

It's an ancient Chinese custom that if you saved someone's life, you were forever responsible for them. I understood that. I suppose, in a way, I felt that way about Nicole. I loved her. But I wasn't *in* love with her. That's not to say I couldn't be. Maybe I just didn't know. I hadn't yet hung a vacancy sign on my heart.

And then there was Falene. My feelings for Falene were as complex as the changes in my world. Falene was more than beautiful and loyal: she was my one constant—the safe ground in the emotional tsunami in my life.

My feelings for both women were confusing and, perhaps, moot. I still didn't know whether or not I was going to live.

I climbed out of bed and walked to the bathroom. It had been a while since I had looked at myself in the mirror and I looked about as rough as I had expected. My skin was dark with tan and dirt and my jaw was covered with a fresh beard. My hair was long and as tangled as a rat's nest.

On a metal shelf above the bathroom sink was a personal hygiene kit with a plastic comb, a disposable razor and a small travel-size can of Barbasol shaving cream. I lathered up my face, then, stroke after stroke, shaved off my beard. I turned on the shower. I hadn't showered since Hannibal, and the warm water felt marvelous as it washed away several days of grime, coalescing in a steady stream of dirty water on the floor pan. The shower had a retractable seat and I adjusted the shower head, then sat down and bowed my head beneath the stream, letting the water flow over me. Fifteen minutes later I got out and toweled off. I pulled on some fresh underwear and pants, then opened the bathroom door to let the steam out.

"I'm out here," my father said.

He was sitting in the same chair he had occupied the day before, again wearing the same clothes as before.

"Morning," I said.

"Good morning. How are you feeling?"

"Good," I said.

"The nurse said the doctor was going to drop by before we left."

"Nicole told me."

"I didn't see Nicole."

"She went to get me some breakfast." I toweled off my hair, then combed it back and came out of the bathroom. I dug through my pack for a clean shirt.

"Our flight leaves at twelve twenty-seven," my father said. "We should be at the airport at least an hour early, so we should leave here by ten-thirty. That leaves us fifty-seven minutes to get to the airport."

My father was crazily precise about numbers. I had wondered before whether his obsession came from years of accounting or if he was just born that way and it led him to accounting. Cause or effect.

"How long ago did Nicole leave?" he asked.

I buttoned up my shirt. "About a half hour. She should be back soon."

"She's a great gal," my father said. "I've enjoyed helping her with her finances."

I was getting a pair of socks from my pack when a wave of nausea swept over me. I grabbed the plastic tub they'd given me to vomit in and leaned over the bed.

"You okay?"

It was a moment before I answered. "Yeah. Still nauseous."

It was a couple minutes before the nausea passed and I set down the tub. "Have you heard from Falene this morning?"

"She left," he said.

I looked up at him. "Left? Where?"

"She went home. She left last night."

I looked at him in disbelief. "Without saying goodbye?"

"She asked me to say goodbye for her."

"I don't understand."

Just then Nicole walked into the room carrying a plastic tray crowded with food. "You're up," she said brightly.

"Mostly," I said.

I looked at the tray.

"I know it's a lot. But the pancakes and waffles both looked good, so I got you both. I also got you a side of bacon. I thought you needed the protein." She turned to my father. "Good morning, Mr. Christoffersen."

"Good morning, Nicole," he replied.

Nicole set the tray down next to my bed. She poured the cranberry juice into a glass of ice, then handed it to me. "Here you go."

"Thank you."

She sat down. "Did the doctor come by?"

"Not yet," I said. I sat down on the side of the bed.

"You look a little pale," Nicole said.

"He just had another bout of nausea," my father replied.

"I'm feeling better," I said.

I poured syrup on the waffles and began to eat. I was halfway through breakfast when the doctor walked into the room.

"Good morning, everyone. How are you feeling, Alan?"

"A little dizzy."

He nodded. "Like I said yesterday, you can expect that to continue until the tumor's removed. We've contacted the cancer center at the UCLA hospital and they have you registered into their system. You have an appointment scheduled for tomorrow morning. I've sent over your files, including your MRI, so they are just awaiting your arrival."

"That's fast," my father said.

He smiled. "I've got some pull. And I have more good news. I spoke with Dr. Schlozman last night and he's agreed to take you on. You're very fortunate to get him. If I had a brain tumor, he's the one I'd go to. But I should warn you, he's a little . . . interesting. He might take a little getting used to."

"Arrogant?" I asked.

Dr. Kelson grinned. "No, not that. He's just quirky. Don't worry about it."

"Thank you, Doctor," I said.

"No problem. Do you have any questions?"

I shook my head. No one else spoke.

"All right, then have a safe flight home. Good luck, Mr. Christoffersen. I hope you're back on the road soon."

"Thank you," I said. "So do I."

"Let's just get you better," my father said. "We can worry about this walking jazz later."

CHAPTER

Four

I've never before realized that it's a privilege to be allowed to make up for the hurt we've done in our lives. This is most evident to me now that I have broken a heart and not been allowed to pick up the pieces.

Alan Christoffersen's diary

A half hour later I checked out of the hospital. Nicole's flight to Spokane was scheduled to leave three hours after our flight to Los Angeles, so we said goodbye in the hospital lobby and she went back to her hotel while my father and I took a taxi to the airport.

The St. Louis airport has notoriously slow security and I had another bout of nausea as I was going through the security line. I threw up on the floor outside the security stanchions, which created no small stir.

My father helped relieve some of my embarrassment by loudly announcing, "He has a brain tumor," which had the remarkable effect of turning everyone instantly sympathetic. More than a dozen people wished me well.

After we had boarded the plane and settled into our seats, I took the airsickness bag from the pouch in front of me and opened it on my lap.

Even with everything I had to think about, Falene's abrupt departure weighed heaviest on my mind. Once we were in the air, I asked my father, "Did Falene say anything before she left?"

My father reached into his carry-on bag and brought out an envelope. "She asked me to give you this. I wanted to wait until we were alone."

I extracted from the envelope an ivory-colored card embossed with an iridescent foil seashell. Inside the card was a folded square of papers. My name was written on it in Falene's handwriting. I unfolded the pages and began to read.

My dear Alan,

Sometimes a girl can be pretty deaf to the things she doesn't want to hear. I should have heard your answer in your silence. I've asked you twice if I could be there when you arrived in Key West and you never answered me. I should have known that was my answer. If you had wanted me there, you would have answered with a loud "yes." Forgive me for being so obtuse (I learned that word from you). But there's a good reason I ignored the obvious. The truth was too painful. You see, I love you. I'm sorry that you had to learn it here, so far from me. I looked forward to the day when I could say it to your face. But I now know that day will never come.

I love you. I know this. I really, truly, deeply love you. I first realized that I had fallen in love with you about two months after I started working at the agency.

Of course, I wasn't alone. I think all the women at your agency had a crush on you. Why wouldn't they? You were handsome and funny and smart, but most of all, you had a good heart.

Truthfully, you seemed too good to be true. You were also loyal to your wife, which made you even more desirable.

Up until I met you, I thought all men were users and abusers. Then you had to come along and ruin my perfect misandry. You are everything a man should be. Strong but gentle, smart but kind, serious but fun, with a great sense of humor. In my heart I fantasized about a world where you and I could be together. How happy I would be to call you mine!!

I know this will sound silly and juvenile, like a schoolgirl crush, but I realized that your name is in my name. You are the AL in FALENE. (As you can see, I've spent way too much time fantasizing about you!) But that's all it was. Fantasy.

When McKale died, I was filled with horrible sadness and concern for you. I was afraid that you might hurt yourself. Seeing the pain you felt made my love and respect for you grow even more. Please forgive me, but the afternoon of the funeral, when I brought you home, I believed, or hoped, for the first time, that someday you might be mine. I didn't feel worthy of you, but I thought that you, being who you are, might accept me.

When you told me you were going to walk away

from Seattle, I was heartbroken. I was so glad that you asked me to help you, giving me a way to stay in your life. Then, when you disappeared in Spokane, I was terrified. I didn't sleep for days. I spent nearly a hundred hours hunting you down. I'm not telling you this so you'll thank me; I just want you to finally know the truth about the depth of my feelings.

But, like I said, a girl can be pretty deaf sometimes. I wanted to hear you say that you loved me and cared about me as more than just a friend. Yesterday, when I saw how close you are to beautiful Nicole, my heart broke. I realized that I had already lost my one chance of being yours. And there I was with nothing to offer. Not even my apartment in Seattle to go to anymore.

I didn't tell you, but I took the job in New York. I needed to get out of Seattle. I failed to save my brother. I failed to save your agency. I failed to make you love me. I've failed at everything I've hoped for.

I'm sorry I didn't finish the task you gave me. I gave all your banking information to your father. He'll do a better job than I could anyway. I'm so sorry to not be at your side in your time of need, but it is now obvious to me that you don't need me. I'm just noise in the concert of your life. And this time I need to be selfish. I have to be. The risk to my heart is too great. They say that the depth of love is revealed in its departure. How true that is. I'm afraid that I'm just learning how deep my love is for you, and it's more than I can stand. I love you too much to just be a bystander in your life.

Well, I guess I've finally burned the bridge. I couldn't help myself. Please forgive me for being so needy. Please think of me fondly and now and then remember your starry-eyed assistant who loves you more than anything or anyone else in this world.

I know you will reach Key West. I know you'll make it and that you'll be okay. That's all I need. It's not all I want, but it's all I need— to know that you are okay and happy. Damn, I really love you.

Be safe, my dear friend. With all my love,
Falene

I put the letter down, mechanically folding the pages back together. Falene was right. The depth of love is revealed in its departure, because my heart ached. *How could I have taken her so much for granted?* I had been so obsessed with my pain that I had been oblivious to hers. She had given me her heart and I had handled it carelessly. I had thrown away love.

CHAPTER

Five

Roses can grow in slums just as weeds
can grow around mansions.

Alan Christoffersen's diary

Even though we had met in Seattle, Falene and I were both raised in California. Same state, but different worlds. While I was raised in a relatively prosperous suburb of Pasadena, home of the Rose Bowl, Caltech, and Fuller Theological Seminary, Falene was born and raised north of me in Stockton, California, a city ranking among California's top ten in crime and listed as number two in *Forbes* magazine's list of America's Most Miserable Cities.

Her home life was as broken as the city. Not that it was apparent from knowing her. The Falene I first met was kind and beautiful, but guarded. It took many months before she revealed any of what lay behind her psychological curtain.

Falene knew little about her father other than that the last time she saw him was right before her brother was born and that he was of Greek descent, something she was reminded of every time she looked in the mirror. Her mother was an alcoholic. Falene's brother, Deron, was five years younger than her and her only sibling, though, in many respects, he was more like Falene's child, as she had been his primary caregiver for most of his childhood. By the age of nine she was collecting shopping carts at a nearby Safeway for a dime apiece, to help buy food. It was all she could do to keep child welfare from splitting up her family.

How two people raised in the same environment can turn out so differently, I'll never understand. According to Falene, Deron had started drinking by the age of ten, smoking pot by eleven and joined a Stockton street gang by thirteen, when he began both using and selling harder drugs.

Falene's mother passed away from alcohol poisoning when Falene was eighteen. Two days after the funeral, Falene packed what she could in the back of her mother's Dodge Dart, forced Deron into the passenger seat of the car, and didn't stop driving until eight hundred miles later when they reached the outskirts of Seattle.

Falene had chosen Seattle because she had a former boyfriend who had moved there the year before, and even though he was ten years older than her and frequently abusive, he had offered Falene a place to stay while they made a new start.

Falene was always a little vague (and embarrassed) when she talked about her early days in Seattle, though once, during a difficult time, she told me that before she started working as a model, she had worked three months at a strip club to make enough money to take care of Deron. It was a humiliating secret, and she was certain I would look down on her, but the truth is I admired her for sacrificing so much to take care of her brother.

Thankfully, Falene was one blessing that Kyle couldn't take away from me. Even though it was he who had discovered her on a model shoot and offered her the job, she had a battle-earned instinct about men and from the beginning never trusted him.

Of necessity, Falene was pretty hard in those early

days, and I watched her change—first her wardrobe and vocabulary, then her demeanor. She became soft and polished, shedding the skin of her past with the graceful ease of a woman coming to her true self. She was just naturally good. She began studying yoga and the Bible and began asking me questions about God, which I could never answer.

Falene had been the one to tell me that McKale had been in an accident. She was also the only one on my staff who had stood up to Kyle as he stole my agency, and she'd tried to warn me about his treachery. She had watched over me and taken me home the afternoon of McKale's funeral when I was in emotional shambles. She had personally overseen the selling of all of my things and put the money in an account to fund my walk. She had always been there, asking for nothing in return. Besides my father, she was the only person I knew I could trust my life to. And when you find someone in your life like that, you're a fool to let them go.

Apparently, I was a fool.

CHAPTER

Six

I've returned to my childhood home. Little
has changed, including my father. I don't
mean this derogatively. In a tumultuous
sea a small anchor goes a long way.

Alan Christoffersen's diary

Our flight to LAX was broken up by a layover in Cincinnati. The moment my father and I exited the jetway, I took out my phone and dialed Falene's number. It rang once, followed by a phone service message.

We're sorry, the number you have dialed is no longer in service.

After we'd sat down, my father said, "Falene?"

"She's disconnected her phone. I have no idea where to find her." I looked at my father. "She didn't leave you any contact information?"

"No. Don't you know where she lives?"

"Not anymore. She moved to New York City."

"How hard could it be to find her there?"

I looked at him. "You're kidding, right?"

He nodded. "Yeah." After a moment he said, "I'm surprised that you didn't see it."

I glanced up at him. "See what?"

"That she loves you."

"I wasn't looking," I said.

My father looked at me thoughtfully. "Don't be too hard on yourself. I don't know if you remember, but for

Grandpa's seventieth birthday he went back to Utah Beach to see where he had fought on D-Day. Do you know what struck him as most peculiar about the experience? He said, 'I never noticed how beautiful the beach was. I guess a million bullets will change your perspective.' "

"No one's firing bullets at me," I said.

"Don't kid yourself, you've had your own war. With casualties."

I shook my head. "I just can't even think about replacing McKale."

"No, no one can replace McKale. And trying to do so would only bring misery. There's only one reason for remarrying." He held up his index finger. "Just one."

"Love?" I said.

"Joy. You marry because it enhances joy."

I thought over his words. "I just feel so selfish. I've been so consumed with my pain that I . . ."

My father put his hand on my knee. "Cut yourself some slack, son. You're entitled."

"To what? Self-pity?"

"No," he said firmly. "To your grief. Grief isn't a luxury, it's an appropriate response to loss. You don't just will it away. If you allow it to run its course, it will fade with time, but if you ignore it or pretend it doesn't exist, it only gets worse."

I breathed out slowly. "I guess so."

"May I give you some advice?"

"Sure."

"Let it settle. You don't know if Falene will change her mind and come back. And we still don't know how bad this tumor is. Let's focus on one problem at a time."

"All right," I said. "That's good advice."

My father looked content. Few things pleased him more than people liking his advice.

.✳.

I started feeling dizzy again, so I took a Dramamine and slept through the entire next leg of our flight, which touched down in LAX around six o'clock. We picked up our luggage, then I waited with it at the curb while my father brought his car around. We stopped on the way home at a Jack in the Box. I wasn't hungry, so my father ordered his meal to go. Then we continued on to the house of my youth.

> Even without her, McKale's home is still a
> memorial to my first and only love.

Alan Christoffersen's diary

I hadn't been back to Pasadena for more than four years. I was surprised by the depth of emotion I felt at seeing McKale's childhood home next door. The house looked serene and unchanged, as if no one had informed it that its former occupant had passed away.

My father carried my pack to the guest room. "I think you should stay here," he said. "It's bigger than your old room. And it's got the connected bathroom. This way I'll be close if you need anything."

"Thank you," I said.

"Can I get you anything now?"

"Dad, I'm home. I can take care of myself."

"Right. Sorry." He carried his hamburger into the front room. "I'm going to watch some TV. They're re-airing the

'74 Ali and Foreman title fight. The Rumble in the Jungle.
You're welcome to join me."

Out of habit, I stopped in the kitchen and lifted the lid
of the cookie jar, but there was nothing inside. Probably
hadn't been for a decade. "The Rumble in the Jungle?"

"You haven't seen it?"

"Nineteen seventy-four? I wasn't born yet."

"Great. You can bet on Foreman. I'll give you a million-
to-one odds."

"That's very generous," I said. "Let me put some laundry
in first."

"Let me—"

I raised my hand. "I got it, Dad."

"I was just going to say I need to empty the dryer."

"I'll take care of it. Eat your burger and watch your fight."

✦

I retrieved my pack, dumped the contents on the laundry
room floor, then put my whites in the washing machine
and went to the front room. A crescent of a hamburger
was lying on its wrapper on the end table next to my father's La-Z-Boy chair and he was eating a bowl of mint
chocolate chip ice cream. In spite of all the internal tur-
moil I felt, or perhaps because of it, the scene made me
smile. My father was a man of habit. He had the same
routine when I was a boy—TV and a bowl of mint chocolate chip ice cream.

I got myself a bowl of ice cream, then sat down on the
sofa. The fight was in its third round. Truthfully, watching two guys pound each other when your own head is
aching isn't terribly amusing. During the sixth round the
washing machine's timer buzzed and I got up.

"I'm going to finish my laundry," I said. "Then go to bed."

My father didn't look up. "We need to leave tomorrow a little before nine. We're going to hit traffic."

"I'll be ready."

I moved my wet clothes to the dryer, put my darks into the washing machine, then went to my room. I didn't sleep well and got up the next morning around 5 A.M. I went down the hall to my childhood bedroom, which looked exactly the way I had left it fifteen years earlier, with my Jurassic Park, U2 and Red Hot Chili Peppers posters still on the wall.

On top of my dresser was a sizable cluster of prom pictures of McKale and me. With the exception of one girls'-preference dance during my junior year, McKale was the only one I had gone with to the school proms.

I sat down on the avocado-colored shag carpeted floor in front of my bookshelf, and pulled out my high school yearbooks and began leafing through the pages. In my senior yearbook there was a picture of McKale and me eating lunch together in the school cafeteria with a caption underneath that read "Most Likely to Marry," which, like the "Most Likely to Succeed" nod, is usually a harbinger of future disaster, but in our case was prophetic.

✦

My father got up an hour later. He went out for his daily two-mile jog, then did calisthenics in the garage. When he'd finished exercising, he showered and dressed, then came out to the kitchen and made oatmeal. The doctor hadn't said whether or not I should eat anything, so I skipped breakfast.

We left for the hospital at a quarter of nine. The registration process was interminable, and it was an hour and a half before I met my neurosurgeon, Dr. Schlozman, a bald, skinny man wearing a bright red bow tie. He greeted us warmly as he walked into the room.

"Sorry for the wait. You'd think that foursome in front of us had never golfed before." He reached out his hand. "I'm Dr. Schlozman."

I smiled. "I'm Alan."

"I'm Alan's father," my dad said.

"Nice to meet you both—let's jump into this." He turned back toward a series of MRI scans posted on light boxes mounted on the wall. "According to exhibit A, you have a tumor." He set his finger on a golf-ball-sized mass on the film. ". . . Either that or you've got a golf ball growing on the outside of your brain." He turned back and looked at me. "I don't know how much they told you in St. Louis, or, with their accents, how much you actually understood, so I'll begin from the beginning. The twenty-four-thousand-dollar question is, 'Is this tumor malignant or benign?' And the answer is, I don't know. We can't be certain without a biopsy." He turned back to the image, running his finger along its edge. "Meningiomas are classified by where they are located. As you can see, yours is located on the surface of the brain— it's called a convexity meningioma. If it were located in New York, it would be called a book agent, but we'll stick with your scenario.

"Your type of tumor often doesn't produce symptoms until it gets big, which is, holy cow, exactly what you've got going on in your head. I read in the Cliff's Notes that you've been suffering from headaches and dizziness—is that true?"

"Pretty much every day," I said.

"Which is why five out of five doctors would recommend a craniotomy as the next step. The good news is that because of the tumor's shape and location I believe we can remove it safely in a procedure called a gross total resection, which is appropriately named because it is totally gross. Trust me, you don't want a souvenir video. The surgery will relieve the pressure on your brain, which should alleviate your symptoms. This procedure has a very high success rate and afterwards you'll be able to continue on with your life *and* play the piano."

I could tell his personality was off-putting to my father, but I liked him a lot.

"Will I need radiation or chemotherapy afterwards?" I asked.

"If the tumor's completely resected, then there's no need for further treatments. That's not to say you're forever home free. After surgery it's best that we monitor the area with periodic MRIs. Like crazy ex-girlfriends, meningiomas have a nasty habit of coming back, so it's best if you have annual scans throughout your life."

"This craniotomy," my father said. "Does it have any risks?"

"No surgery's without risk, but in this case the risks are quite minimal. The greatest risk, though it's about as likely as me finding true love, is stroke. Also, some neurological functions like motor strength or coordination may become impaired immediately after surgery, but in most cases those issues are resolved with time and rehabilitation." He turned to me. "Mostly you'll just feel really, really crappy for a while."

"How soon could we do this?" I asked.

"The soonest we can schedule your operation is the

nineteenth. Then you'll need to plan for at least six to eight weeks of recovery time."

"Six weeks," I repeated. I hated the idea of that much downtime, but it could be worse. I had spent nearly five months recovering at Nicole's house.

"Six to eight," my father said. "At least."

"All right," I said. "Let's do this thing."

"Good," Dr. Schlozman said. "I was hoping you'd say that. I've been looking at a new boat."

The drive home from the hospital was quiet. My father was the first to speak. "That doctor was weird."

"I looked up his credentials. He's brilliant," I said. "Brilliant people usually are a little weird."

He shrugged. "Want to stop for pancakes? The IHOP is still there."

"Love to. Let's get pancakes."

CHAPTER

Seven

Sometimes it seems as if my life has
been more intermission than show.

Alan Christoffersen's diary

Nicole called the house later that afternoon. It was good to hear her voice.

"Hey, handsome. How'd your appointment go?"

"Well, I think. They're going to operate on the nineteenth."

"Why are they waiting so long?"

"That's their first availability."

"Then how long is your recovery?"

"Six to eight weeks," I said. "If everything goes well."

"I'm sure it will go well," she said. "But you'll go insane waiting."

"Probably."

"So, may I come down and take care of you?" she asked. "Please."

"I would love for you to come," I said. "When are you thinking?"

"I'd like to come before the surgery. How about the sixteenth? Two weeks from today."

"That would be great," I said. "Now I have something to look forward to."

"Me too," she said.

We talked for a few more minutes before saying goodbye.

My father walked into the room after I hung up. "Was that Nicole?"

"Yes. She wants to come down for the surgery."

"What did you say?"

"I told her I'd love to see her." I frowned. "Do you think I'm leading her on?"

"She's a friend and she cares. Where's the crime in that?"

I shrugged. "I just don't want to hurt her. She means too much to me."

"She's a big girl," he said. "When is she coming?"

"The sixteenth."

He nodded. "It will be nice having a woman around."

✦

The next two weeks were miserable. As my surgery date neared, I started sleeping more—sometimes as much as fourteen hours a day. Dr. Schlozman had warned me that I would likely become more fatigued, but I think it was more than the tumor. I was also fighting depression. There was just too much around to remind me of McKale, too much time to think, and too little to do. You don't realize how many memories of someone a place can hold until they're gone.

My dizzy spells and headaches were increasing in frequency and duration, and I began to have trouble walking. Still, I hated lying in bed. My father had an elliptical machine in his garage, which, with some difficulty, I used twice a day, though probably as much out of boredom as a desire to keep active.

My father's routine was as rigid as it had been when I was a boy. We ate dinner every night at six-thirty sharp, followed by dishwashing, then television in the family room with his customary bowl of mint chocolate chip ice cream.

There was one gradual and unwelcome change to our routine. Every night during dinner, when I was captive at the table, my father began pressing me with questions about my future, specifically my employment. He asked whether or not I was going to stay in advertising, if I planned to work for another firm or start a new agency, and if I would accept investors. "I know money people," he said on more than one occasion.

With his typical fastidiousness he would verbally walk me through a list of pros and cons for each option. Then, during his free time, he began searching the Internet for job openings at Los Angeles agencies and writing down their phone numbers just in case I wanted to "test the waters."

For several days he got on a kick about me getting a car, which he offered to buy even though I was in no condition to drive. Although I appreciated his support, I knew what he was doing. He was trying to nail me down.

I suppose just as telling was what he never talked about. He never mentioned McKale, and he never talked about my walk. I could understand why he wouldn't bring up McKale. But I couldn't understand why he wouldn't talk about my journey. There was so much to talk about.

From all appearances he resented my walk even though he had endorsed it back in Spokane.

I humored him through it all, but it seemed that each dinner got gradually more uncomfortable. Nicole couldn't get here soon enough.

The day of Nicole's arrival I moved my things to my childhood room so she could have her own bathroom. We picked her up at the airport around three in the afternoon. After our reunion, I began feeling unwell, so my father drove me home, then the two of them went shopping for dinner.

I had forgotten what a good cook Nicole was. She made broiled salmon with polenta and acorn squash soup. Dessert was a lemon meringue pie from the Marie Callender's in Arcadia.

Somewhat surprising was that my father, who drank as infrequently as I did, opened a bottle of Chardonnay. I couldn't remember the last time I'd seen him that happy or loose.

Later, after my father had gone to bed, Nicole knocked on my bedroom door. "It's me," she said softly.

I opened. Nicole was wearing sweat pants and a Victoria's Secret PINK T-shirt. She looked cute.

"Come in," I said.

She walked inside, running her hand down my arm as she stepped past me. "Your dad's home is nice," she said. "It's very . . ."

"Seventies?"

She grinned. "I was going to say cozy." She walked over to the window and pulled back the curtain. "Which home did McKale live in?"

"That one," I said, pointing. "The little ranch-style house."

"You married the girl next door." She spotted the prom pictures on my dresser and walked over to them. She lifted one and burst out laughing. "Is this *you*?"

"In my defense, my dad cut my hair back then."

"No, you look great." She looked at the picture, then back at me. "You were adorable as a teenager." She smiled at me. "You still are."

"Thanks."

"And this is McKale?"

"That's McKale."

"She's beautiful." She looked at each of the pictures, stopping at the one odd one. "Who's this?"

"I think her name was Jennifer. Or Jodie. Or Justine. Actually, I have no idea what her name was. That was a girls'-preference dance at another school."

"I take it she didn't get the memo that you were taken?"

"Apparently not. First and last date."

"How did McKale take it, you going out with someone else?"

"She handled it with her usual passive aggressiveness. She said it didn't bother her, then went out on a date the next weekend with some football jock. I think she just wanted to remind me that she had options."

"We girls are like that." She stepped away from the bookshelf. "How is it being back here with your father?"

"It's been difficult. He's made it pretty clear that he wants me to stay."

"Yeah, he told me that while we were shopping. He asked if I'd help talk you into abandoning your walk."

I looked at her and frowned. "He really said that?"

She nodded.

"I'm finishing my walk."

"I know. I tried to explain to him how important it is to you." She took my hand. "Don't be angry with him. He's just worried about you. Remember how upset he was when he found out you'd been mugged? And now you have a tumor. You may be over thirty, but he's still your father. And you're the only family he has." She took my hand. "He just cares."

I thought about what she'd said, then breathed out slowly. "I know."

"Other than that, how have you been feeling?"

"It's getting worse," I said. "The doctor said it would."

"I'm sorry."

"It's okay. It will be over soon."

Something about the way I said this affected her. Her eyes welled up.

"What's wrong?" I asked.

She wiped her eyes, then looked into mine. "Sorry. I didn't like how that sounded."

I put my arms around her and she fell into me. I held her for several minutes. Then she leaned back. "I better let you get your rest."

"I'm glad you're here," I said. "Thank you for coming."

"There's no way I was going to let you go through this alone. Besides, I kind of like you."

I smiled. "The feeling's mutual."

"Night," she said. "Sweet dreams."

※

That night I dreamt I was kissing McKale. When I pulled back, it was really Falene.

CHAPTER

Eight

Looking at someone's brain is a little like
looking at the outside of a movie theater.

Alan Christoffersen's diary

The morning of the nineteenth my father drove us to the hospital several hours before my scheduled surgery time, so we'd have plenty of time to wind our way through the labyrinth of admissions. After filling out a pile of forms, we sat in the waiting room for nearly an hour before I was called to the preoperative holding area, where they put me in one of those ill-fitting, tie-in-back gowns, then sent at least a dozen people in to see me in my humbled state.

"You look cute," Nicole said, lifting her phone. "I'm taking a picture."

"No pictures," I said.

She brought out her phone. "I'm taking one anyway."

"No pictures," I said again.

She snapped a picture. "Too late."

Shortly before surgery a young man came in to shave my head, which, considering the length of my hair, was no simple feat. When he was done, I just stared at myself in the mirror.

"I'm bald."

"As a bowling ball," Nicole said.

"A billiard ball," my father corrected.

"They're both hairless," I said.

"Like you," Nicole said.

"Thanks. Are you going to take another picture?"

"No." She held up a lock of my hair. "But I'm keeping this."

"You know, they didn't have to shave all of it," my dad said. "They could have shaved just one side."

"What do you do with half a head of hair?" I asked. "That's like half a mustache."

"Or one eyebrow," Nicole said. "Then again, you could have had the mother of all comb-overs."

"Being here reminds me of when you were seven," my father said. "You had to get your tonsils out. That used to be considered major surgery."

"I remember," I said. "Mom read me a story about a baby whale. And I got a stuffed Snoopy doll. I wonder what happened to it."

"I probably left it in Colorado," he said.

My father and Nicole were still at my side when the anesthesiologist came in to introduce himself and make sure I was properly prepared for surgery. He told me that they would come for me in five minutes. As he walked out, Nicole began crying.

"What's wrong?" I asked.

"Nothing. I'm just a crybaby. I get so worried."

"Everything is going to be all right," I said.

She wiped her eyes, forcing a smile. "I know."

A few minutes later two surgical techs arrived to take me to the operating room. Nicole kissed me on the cheek. My father, in a rare show of affection, took my hand. "You'll be fine," he said, sounding more as if he were trying to convince himself than comfort me. I think I was the least worried of all of us.

The techs wheeled my entire bed to the operating

room, and Nicole and my father followed me down the hallway until we came to the NO PUBLIC ADMITTANCE doors of the surgical center. Nicole was teary-eyed again and blew me a kiss. I smiled at her and touched my lips.

Once inside the operating room, the anesthesiologist put the mask on my face and told me to count backward from ten. I only made it to nine.

·✻·

When I woke in recovery, my father was sitting by my side. He was reading a *Popular Science* magazine, but set it down when I stirred.

"Welcome back."

My head felt thick and my words came slowly. "Thanks."

"How do you feel?" Nicole asked.

I slowly turned my head to look at her. "My throat hurts."

"That's from the breathing tube," another female voice said. A nurse leaned over me. "Alan, I'm Rachel. I just need to check a few things." She lifted a small flashlight. "Let me have you look forward." She shone the light at my pupils. "Can you tell me what day your birthday is?"

"Are you planning a party?"

She grinned. "At least you haven't lost your sense of humor. Do you know when it is?"

"June fifth," I said.

She looked to my father for verification. He nodded.

"Very good," she said. She got up and walked to the foot of my bed. She lifted the sheet, then cupped my feet with her hands. "I want you to push your feet into my hands."

"Why?"

"Just for fun," she said.

I must have done a good enough job at it because she

wrote something on her clipboard, then left. After she was gone, I turned to my dad. "Do we know the verdict?"

"It's benign," he said.

"Benign. That's the good one, right?"

Nicole laughed. "Yes, it's good."

"Good." I groaned out slowly. "I'm tired."

"The doctor said you'd be out of it most of the day," my father said.

"I think he was right," I said. I fell back asleep.

✦

Dr. Schlozman came in to check on me an hour later. My father stood as he entered.

"It went well," he said to me. "I'm sure they told you the tumor was benign, so we can all high-five, or chest bump, however you want to celebrate."

"Why do I feel so crummy?" I asked.

"I don't know," he said. "Maybe it's because *you just had brain surgery*." He grinned. "You'll feel a little better tomorrow."

"What's next?" my father asked.

"He'll have an MRI in the morning to make sure we got it all, then, if all's well, he heads home on Thursday."

"That soon?" Nicole asked.

"If the MRI checks out, so does he." He smiled at me. "Thanks for staying alive, Alan. It looks good on my résumé."

✦

The rest of the evening I drifted in and out of sleep. When I woke the next morning, I had been given a catheter, something I was always very afraid of. It was an infection caused by her catheter that had killed McKale.

A little before noon, I was taken by wheelchair for an MRI. On my way down the hall I saw myself in the reflection of a window. In addition to being bald, my head was swollen and I had a long row of staples in my scalp, with a deep indentation along the line of the incision. I looked like a monster.

Later in the afternoon I was moved into a private room. Dr. Schlozman came in to see me shortly after lunch.

"I've got great news," he said.

"You got the tumor?" my father asked.

"That too," Dr. Schlozman said. "But *my* good news is that my new book came out today and it's a bestseller on Amazon.com."

I was still a little foggy and wasn't sure I was hearing him right. "You wrote a book?"

"It's called *The Zombie Autopsies*. It's a medical journal about the origin of the zombie virus."

"You wrote a book about zombies?" Nicole asked.

"Yes, and it's currently number fifty-seven on Amazon. Right between David Baldacci and Nicholas Sparks."

My father looked annoyed. "But my son's okay, right?"

Dr. Schlozman waved him off. "He's fine, we got it all. Every crumb of it."

"Thank goodness," Nicole said.

"I still feel crummy," I said.

Dr. Schlozman smiled. "I guess we can't have everything, can we?"

✳

The next morning the nurses prepared for my discharge. They gave my father prescriptions for pain medications and a sheet of instructions for caring for my incision. I just

wanted to lie quietly without distractions—no talk, television or reading. It was as if words and sounds pricked
my brain.

Around noon an orderly wheeled me out of the hospital and helped me into my father's car. Frankly, I didn't
feel a whole lot better and I felt more tired than I had
the day before. I felt overstimulated by everything around
me. More than anything, I wanted to be left alone.

Through it all Nicole was helpful and kind, but she also
seemed sad. It was nearly a week before I found out why.

✦

Six days after my surgery I was lying in bed when Nicole
came into my room. Her eyes were red and swollen from
crying.

I sat up. "What's wrong?"

She hesitated a moment, then said, "I'm going back to
Spokane."

"I thought you were staying longer."

She avoided eye contact. "I was going to, but I think I
should be going."

"Did I do something wrong?"

"It's not your fault." She took another deep breath.
"When you were in recovery, you kept asking for Falene.
At the time I told myself it was the anesthesia . . ." She
looked me in the eyes. "You love her, don't you?"

I looked down for a moment, then back at her. "I don't
know. I suppose I don't know how deep the waters go,
since I wasn't really fishing."

She was quiet for a moment, then said, "I love you.
Not just because you saved me, but . . ." She took a deep
breath. "I'm sorry. I'm just making this more difficult." She

took my hand. "I'll go." She leaned over and kissed me on the cheek. "Thank you for all you've been to me. I'll always love you."

"Nicole . . ."

She looked at me, but I had no idea what to say. After a moment she said, "It's okay, Alan." She walked out of my room.

Now I'd lost her too.

CHAPTER

Nine

Early the next morning my father drove Nicole to the airport. After he returned, he came into my room.

"Is she okay?" I asked.

"She's hurting. Unrequited love is a painful thing."

"I didn't mean to hurt her. I do love her."

"I know."

I sighed. "Now what do I do?"

He leaned against my wall. "What do you want to do?"

"Since when has that mattered?"

"It's always mattered. It doesn't mean you'll get what you want, but what you want always matters. That's what defines you."

"I want my life back."

"Your life or wife?"

"They're the same thing."

"No, they're not," he said, frowning. "What do you want for your life that's within the realm of possibility?"

"I want to figure out my feelings. I need to talk to Falene. But I don't even know where she is."

"Someone knows where she is."

"That's not helpful," I said.

My father thought a moment, then said, "I have a client who's a private investigator. A few years ago he fell on hard times, and I did his taxes for free. He keeps saying, 'Let me do something for you.' That's his expertise, hunting down people—child support dodgers, bail jumpers, corporate embezzlers. He's darn good, too. I bet he could find Falene."

"What's your friend's name?"

"Carroll Albo."

"Let's give him a call."

✦

That afternoon I spoke with my father's friend Carroll. He didn't sound like I expected him to, though, admittedly, my perception of private investigators was largely shaped by *Columbo* and *Magnum, P.I.* reruns. This man sounded squeaky and timid, more fit for accounting than manhunting and intrigue.

I told him everything I knew about Falene, which wasn't especially helpful. Her past had little to help us in the present.

"You say she got a job with a modeling agency in New York?"

"Yes."

"There's probably a couple hundred of them. At least. We could start looking. What about friends or family? Old boyfriends?"

"Her old boyfriends were all bad news, so she wouldn't have told any of them where she was going. She didn't really have any girlfriends that she hung out with."

"Family?"

"She has an aunt. I've never met her, but she owns a furniture consignment store."

"Do you know her name?"

"No, but I know the store. It's called the Fifth Avenue Consigner. It's in Seattle."

He paused as he wrote it down. "Anyone else?"

"She has a brother. But he's MIA. She doesn't even know where he is."

"Why is that?"

"He was in a gang and messed up with drugs."

"That's not a bad thing," Carroll said. "I mean, it's horrible for him, but for our purposes, it's not bad. What's his name?"

"Deron Angelis."

"Spell it."

"D-e-r-o-n A-n-g-e-l-i-s."

"Got it. Do you know where he spends his time? What city?"

"He used to live with Falene."

"In Seattle?"

"Yes."

"I'll be back with you as soon as I have something."

·✦·

Carroll called just three days later. Truthfully, I hadn't expected to hear from him so soon. A part of me didn't expect to hear from him at all.

"Her aunt's name is Chloe Adamson," Carroll said. "But she doesn't know where Falene is. Or if she does, she's not telling. But I found her brother. Deron Angelis, twenty-three years old, born January 20, 1989, in San Joaquin County."

"How did you find him?"

"Hunting drug addicts and gang members isn't hard.

Eventually they end up in one of three places: hospital, jail or the morgue."

"Which one was it?"

"He's in the King County jail."

"King County?"

"In Seattle. He was caught in possession of meth and was sentenced to prison for several years, but had the sentence suspended. He has to serve a county jail sentence for six months, then when he's released, he'll be on probation for a couple of years."

"I can see him there?"

"Visiting hours are determined by inmate location. I checked on it for you. He's assigned Sundays from noon to one-thirty and Tuesdays from five-thirty to seven."

I wrote down the information.

"In the meantime I'll keep hunting your girl. My secretary has called at least fifty modeling agencies so far, but only found one Falene, and she's from Brazil. Your friend didn't go by a different professional name, did she? You know, like movie stars sometimes do if they don't have a fancy enough name?"

"Falene isn't fancy enough?"

"It is to me, but all my taste's in my mouth."

"Not that I know of. She went by Falene in Seattle."

"Oh, one more thing. I should have asked you last time if you know any of her past employers."

"I'm her past employer," I said.

"Holy cow, why didn't you tell me?"

"I guess I thought you knew."

"No, I didn't. Can you track down her Social Security number?"

"I think so. I just need to call my old accountant."

"That's our golden ticket. As soon as she applies for a job, or welfare benefits, we'll find her."

"I'll track it down," I said. "Thank you."

"Don't mention it. I'm happy to be able to do something for your pop. He's been a lifesaver to me."

"He's a good man," I said.

"You said it. You've got to be grateful for an old man like that. Mine just beat the crap out of me, then threw me out when I was seventeen. You count your blessings."

Within the hour I had Falene's Social Security number, which I passed on to Carroll. He called back a few hours later.

"Nothing on her yet," he said. "But she'll turn up. Unless she's bypassing the system."

"What do you mean?"

"Sometimes people pay under the table."

"Maybe I'll go visit her brother. I can't imagine that she won't be looking for him."

"Good idea," Carroll said. "No stone unturned."

CHAPTER

We have found Falene's brother. I hope
he knows where she is almost as much
as I hope she doesn't know where he is.

Alan Christoffersen's diary

I called the King County jail to confirm Deron's visiting hours, then booked a one-day flight into Seattle for the Sunday after next. I was still struggling with my health and I wanted to be up for the encounter. I also figured this would give Carroll more time to track Falene down and possibly save me the trip.

He didn't find her and nine days later, my father drove me to LAX. The flight into the Sea-Tac airport was around three hours, and I had planned my trip to arrive an hour before visiting hours were scheduled to begin. I had no luggage and took a cab from the airport to the jail. It was surreal being back in Seattle. It was my first time back since I had walked out ten months ago. I had purposely scheduled my return flight for the same day so I would spend as little time in Seattle as possible. I wasn't ready to face all of the memories that the city held for me.

At the jail I went through a security screening into a long, open visiting room. I was given a booth number, then sat down in front of a thick Plexiglas window. I could see my reflection in the glass. I had forgotten how odd I looked—bald-headed with a row of staples running horizontally across my scalp.

Even though I'd never seen Falene's brother before, I

knew it was he when he came into the room. He looked like a male version of Falene. He wasn't big, maybe just a few inches taller than her, and his head was shaved. He had tattoos on his neck of two entwined snakes and Gothic letters, which I guessed spelled out the name of his gang. He was dressed in an orange jumpsuit with his last name printed above his left breast. Even though he was trying to look tough, I could sense his anxiety.

He sat down at a chair on the other side of the window, his dark brown eyes staring into mine. There were phones mounted on the side of the booth next to the window, which we both picked up.

"Who are you?" he asked.

"My name is Alan Christoffersen. I'm a friend of your sister."

"You know Falene?"

"Yes."

"You one of her lowlife boyfriends?"

"No. She used to work for me. At my advertising agency."

"You her boss?"

"I was."

"I know who you are. You're the guy whose stuff I helped Falene move."

I nodded. "Yeah, that was my stuff."

"What happened to your head?"

"I just had a brain tumor removed."

He glanced once more at my head, then said, "What do you want?"

"I'm looking for Falene."

"What's that got to do with me?"

"I was hoping you could help me find her."

"Call her."

"She changed her number."

"She worked for you and you don't know her address?"

"She moved to New York."

He looked surprised. "She doesn't live in New York."

"When was the last time you saw her?" I asked.

"I don't know. A few months ago. Before I came in here."

"She got a job offer from a modeling agency back East. She wasn't going to take it, but after you took off, she gave up."

He flinched. "What do you mean, she gave up?"

"Just what I said. She said she failed with you and gave up."

"Falene never failed at anything."

"She said she failed with you."

In spite of his practiced defiance, he actually looked upset. Finally he stammered out, "What I do with my life has nothing to do with her."

"Do you really believe that? She picked up her life and moved here to keep you out of trouble."

"You don't know anything about me."

"I don't know anything about you except that you've brought Falene a lot of pain."

He slammed the glass barrier. "I love my sister."

"I can see that," I said. "Your sister has done everything she could to help you and you repay her by breaking her heart."

He pounded the window again.

"Deron!" a guard shouted. "Knock it off."

"What do you want?" he said. "You came here to tell me that?"

"I came here to see if you knew how to find her."

"I'm in jail. How would I know how to find her? Why

didn't she tell you where she was going? She like worshiped you."

I felt ashamed to hear that. "I don't know."

"Maybe she doesn't want to see you. Maybe *you're* the reason she left."

"Maybe," I said. "She's been carrying a lot of people by herself for a long time. Maybe she just hit her limit. If you love her, now's a good time to start showing her."

I expected another outburst. Instead he looked down for a moment, then to my surprise said, "Thanks for looking out for her. She deserves that. If I hear from her, I'll let her know you came by."

"Thank you," I said. I hung up the phone and walked out of the room.

※

My flight arrived back in Los Angeles that evening at eight. The effects of my surgery were exacerbated by my traveling, and I was feeling so exhausted I wasn't sure I could make it through the terminal. Gratefully, my father picked me up at the terminal curb.

"How'd it go?" he asked as I climbed into the car.

"He was no help at all."

"Sorry," he said. A moment later he asked, "What was he like?"

I reclined my seat. "Nothing like Falene. Nothing at all."

CHAPTER

Eleven

I've read that there are specific,
predictable stages of grief. But there
must be as many manifestations of
those stages as there are bereft.

Alan Christoffersen's diary

Over the next few weeks I was hoping to hear from Carroll about Falene, but he never called. Physically, I was getting stronger, though my recovery was coming slower than I had hoped, and I was tired most of the time. Emotionally, I was depressed. Sitting in one place made it easy for all my negative thoughts to circle and land on me, like flies on roadkill. All I could think about was getting back out on the road.

Three weeks after my surgery I went back to the hospital to have my staples removed, which I expected to be painful, but the skin around my incision was still numb from where the nerves had been cut and I felt no pain. The next day I began walking again. I started at two miles, then, a week later, increased to three, then four. The dizziness was gone. I still got occasional headaches, but that, and exhaustion, seemed to be the extent of my complications.

A month after my surgery I went back again to see Dr. Schlozman. After telling me a pretty funny joke about Superman in a bar, he gave me a clean bill of health and we scheduled my next MRI for a year out. That afternoon I started making plans to return to the road.

✦

A couple nights later, at dinner, my father said, "I noticed you had your maps out."

I looked up at him. He had been strangely quiet all afternoon, like he was brooding. I finally understood why. "Yes, I was planning my route."

"Then you're going back out after all."

"That was always the plan."

I couldn't read his expression. "When are you leaving?"

"August thirtieth," I said.

"That's next week."

"It's next Tuesday."

He was quiet for a moment, then said, "Are you up to it?"

"I'm not all the way back, but Dr. Schlozman didn't see any problem with it."

He pushed his plate away, then said, "I don't understand why you're doing this. Why not just stay here and get on with your life?"

"Right now the walk is my life."

"Walking is no life," he said. "It's just walking."

"What about what you said on the way here? You said I'm entitled to my own grief, and that I need to allow it to run its course."

"Yes, but allowing it to run its course doesn't mean running from it."

"I'm not running from my grief. Believe me, it follows me every step of the way."

"And that's a good thing?"

"You said in Spokane that you understood why I needed to do this."

"I understood why you left. But it's been almost a year. I don't understand what you hope to accomplish by this."

"I'm not trying to accomplish anything." I looked at him. "Or maybe I am. I can't explain why it's so important. I just know that I need to finish what I started."

For a moment he didn't say anything. Then he shook his head. "It just doesn't make any sense to me."

"But it does to me. And that's what matters. You need to let me deal with my grief the way I need to deal with it."

"But you're not dealing with it. You're running away from it. No, you're *walking* away from it."

"So let me *not* deal with it the way I need to."

He breathed out in exasperation.

"Dad, you know what I'm going through. After Mom died, didn't you want to just escape?"

"I had you," he said. "I couldn't just walk away from everything."

"But did you want to?"

He looked at me for a moment, then stood and took his plate over to the sink. Then he went to his bedroom and shut the door.

I just sat alone at the table. *Is there anyone else I can run out of my life?*

CHAPTER

Twelve

You should always be careful
of what you say in parting.

Alan Christoffersen's diary

Over the next week my father didn't say much—at least not about my leaving. As the time for my departure neared, things between us became increasingly tense, which I dealt with by walking more. Two days before my flight back to St. Louis, my father and I were eating dinner when I just couldn't stand the silence anymore.

"My flight's Tuesday morning," I said.

He kept on eating, meticulously cutting off bite-sized pieces of flank steak, then spearing them and putting them into his mouth.

I breathed out in exasperation. "Dad, I'm leaving. Can we talk about this?"

He kept at his steak. "You've made up your mind. What's there to talk about?"

"Can we talk about why you're so angry?"

He looked me in the eyes. "Do you think that there's something magical about Key West? That the moment you reach the city line your life will just miraculously change and everything will be good again?"

"No, Dad, everything will *never* be good again."

He shook his head. "You need to have faith," he said.

"Faith in what?"

"That life is still worth living."

"What did you think, that I was going to come home and abandon my walk?"

My father's demeanor softened. "No. But I was hoping."

I exhaled slowly, regaining my composure. "Look, I'm sorry. I know you want me to stay. But it's not my path. At least not yet."

"If not now, when?"

I looked at him for a moment, then said, "As soon as I figure that out, I'll let you know." The room fell into silence. Finally, I pushed back from the table. "I'm not hungry." I got up and went to my room.

✦

The next morning I woke with a headache, which I hid from my father at breakfast. Most people would think it strange that we didn't say a thing about our previous night's conversation, but that was predictable. It's just the way we communicated. Or didn't.

Around noon my headache eased some and I walked two miles to the grocery store for supplies, then returned home and laid out my clothes for packing. I felt more alone than I had on the road. I desperately wanted to talk to someone. But Falene was still a vapor and I didn't dare call Nicole.

I called Carroll to see if he had any news about Falene. He had nothing new to report but said he hadn't given up. I told him I was leaving and gave him my cell phone number in case he found her. To my surprise, Nicole called later that afternoon.

"Hey," she said softly. "How are you?"

"I'm so glad you called," I said. "I've missed you."

"Me too," she said. There was a long pause. "So you're leaving tomorrow?"

"You've been talking to my dad?"

"He's my accountant," she said. "We talk every week."

"He's pretty upset."

"I know."

There was another long pause.

"I've managed to run off everyone I love," I said.

"Maybe we just all love you too much."

"Then I could use a little less love about now."

She laughed. "I'm sorry," she said. "I kind of screwed things up between us."

"No you didn't. There's nothing you could do to make me not care about you."

"Thank you," she said. "I feel the same way about you." She breathed out into the mouthpiece. "Are you feeling okay?"

"Emotionally or physically?"

"Let's stick to physically."

"I'm really tired. I still get headaches."

"Maybe you should wait a few more weeks before walking again."

"I can't. I'm going crazy here."

"I know. But you need to be careful. I don't want to hear about any more hospital visits."

"I'll be careful. And I think that getting away from here will help. I need to reboot myself, you know?"

"Yeah, but you be careful out there. And if you ever need anything, call. I don't care what time it is. You know I mean that."

"Thank you."

"Is there anything I can do for you right now?"

"You can look out for my dad."

"Gladly," she said. "He's a good man."

"I know," I said. "Thanks for calling. It's really good talking to you."

"You're welcome. It's good talking to you too. Let's talk again soon."

"I'd like that," I said.

"Alan."

"Yes?"

"I love you."

"I love you too," I replied. I hung up the phone and went back to packing.

✦

To avoid a repeat of the previous night's dinner, I made myself a tuna fish sandwich, then sequestered myself in my room. Later that evening my father knocked at my door.

"Come in," I said.

He stepped inside. "I made tacos," he said.

"Thanks. I already ate."

"I know. I wrapped up two tacos in foil in case you get hungry later. They're in the refrigerator."

"Thank you," I said.

He just stood there, nervously swaying. "What time does your flight leave tomorrow?"

"Ten-thirty."

"Then we should leave by eight-fifteen. We're going to hit rush-hour traffic."

"You don't have to take me," I said. "I can take a cab."

"You're not taking a cab. We'll have breakfast at seven-thirty. Okay?"

"Okay."

He walked out of my room.

❋

The next morning we shared a long, quiet breakfast together. It was one of my father's specialties, Swedish pancakes with lingonberries and pork sausage. I suppose he had made a statement by making one of my favorites. After breakfast I finished packing, then my father drove me to the Los Angeles airport. We said two words on the way. Literally.

"United?"

"Delta."

He pulled up to the Delta curb and put the car in park. I got out and pulled my pack from the back seat. My father got out of the car. His eyes were red.

"You got everything?"

"Yeah." I walked over to him, leaning my pack against the Buick. "Thank you for everything."

He just nodded.

I exhaled heavily. "I love you, Dad."

His eyes welled up, which I knew made him uncomfortable. He leaned forward for a quick hug, then stepped back and, without a word, gently squeezed my shoulder.

I picked up my pack and walked back to the curb. I was near the airport door when my father shouted, "Hey, Al."

I turned back.

"Be safe."

I smiled, then waved and went in to catch my flight.

CHAPTER

Thirteen

I am back in St. Louis. I was so intent on
resisting my father's attempts to abort my
walk that I ignored my own body's warnings.

Alan Christoffersen's diary

After a ninety-minute layover in Detroit, I arrived in St. Louis too late in the day to start walking. I took the hotel shuttle from the airport to the Hyatt Regency at the Arch and planned for a restful evening. I still didn't feel well and I was worried by how much the flight had wearied me. My recovery wasn't nearly as complete as I had led myself to believe. This shouldn't have surprised me. Dr. Schlozman had warned me that it could take as long as six months before I felt like myself again. I just hadn't wanted to hear it.

My room was on the east side of the hotel and had a view of the Arch. The sun, now in the west, gleamed off the monument's stainless-steel surface, making it almost too bright to look at.

The Gateway Arch is one of America's most spectacular national monuments, and a symbol of the western expansion of the United States. A national contest was held in 1947–48, and Finnish-American Eero Saarinen's design was chosen from more than 170 entries. Construction began on the memorial in 1963 and was finished two and a half years later. The Arch is a remarkable feat of engineering and, at 630 feet tall, the tallest man-made monument in the United States—nearly 100 feet taller than the

Washington Monument and almost 70 feet taller than the Crazy Horse Memorial in South Dakota.

For several minutes I lay back in my bed, my gaze fixed on the monument. Even though the Gateway Arch was designed as a symbolic gateway to the West, gates go both ways and it was fitting that I had returned to the Arch after my medical intermission. I had passed the half-way mark of my journey east without fanfare. The Arch made it official—I was on the downhill slope of my walk. But it didn't feel downhill. I felt as if my mountain had only grown steeper.

I rubbed my legs, wondering how my body would hold up on the road. When I was ten, I broke my left arm playing dodgeball at school. When my cast came off, I was surprised at how much smaller my arm looked than the other one and how quickly my muscles had atrophied. As I looked at my calves, I realized how the weeks in Pasadena had taken their toll. Even with my practice walks at home, I doubted I'd make twenty miles my first day. I wondered if I would even make ten. No matter. I wasn't in a race. I closed my eyes and took a nap.

CHAPTER

Fourteen

Everybody needs love. Everybody. Those
who don't believe that frighten me a little.

Alan Christoffersen's diary

My room was dark when I woke. I glanced over at the digital clock: 8:27 P.M. I got out of bed and washed my face with cold water, then took the elevator downstairs to the Ruth's Chris Steak House, which was off the hotel lobby. The restaurant is one of the reasons I had picked the hotel. McKale and I had celebrated our first year of the agency at a Ruth's Chris, along with Kyle Craig and his girlfriend du jour. It was a good time and one I would never forget—an evening of triumph and confidence and gratitude. I remember that McKale looked so incredibly beautiful that night. Indescribably beautiful.

Seeing couples around me in the lobby intensified my memories and my loneliness.

In this setting I understood something. I didn't want to live without McKale. But I also didn't want to live alone. I wasn't born to be celibate. Refusing Analise in Iowa had taken all the strength I had. Everyone needs love. Everyone. And, as my dad was fond of saying, "If you build a fence between a cow and its water, it's going to take down the fence."

Nearly four years ago McKale and I had talked about this very thing on our vacation to Italy. We were on a tour of the Roman Forum, standing near the ruins of the Temple of Vesta, when our guide told us about the three vows made by the Vestal Virgins. First was complete allegiance to the goddess Vesta. Second was a vow to keep the sacred fire of her temple burning. The third was a vow of chastity.

The punishment for breaking the third vow was the most severe. If caught, the male lover would be whipped to death in front of the woman, then she would be wrapped in linen, given a loaf of bread and an oil lantern, then be buried alive.

I asked our guide if, given the extremity of the punishment, any of the Vestal Virgins had ever broken their vow.

"Oh yes," she said solemnly. "Eighteen of them."

"Eighteen!" McKale exclaimed.

"Does this surprise you?" the guide asked in her strong Italian accent. She shook her head. "It does not surprise me. Everyone must have love."

Later that evening, as we stood in front of the Trevi Fountain, McKale asked me something peculiar. "If I were to die, would you remarry?"

I looked at her quizzically. "You're not going to die."

"But if I did, would you remarry?"

"I've never thought about it," I finally said. "I've always assumed I'll die first. Would you?"

"I don't know," she said. "I think I'd probably die of a broken heart."

I smiled and squeezed her hand. A minute later, after we'd started walking again, she said seriously, "If something happens to me, I want you to remarry. I don't want you to live without love."

"Enough of this," I said. "Nothing's going to happen to you."

She stopped and looked up into my eyes with a curious gaze I'll never forget. "You never know," she said.

I wondered what McKale would think of me with Falene. I knew that she liked her, which, frankly, was unusual. Most women took an immediate *dislike* to Falene just because of the way she looked, or, often, because of the way their men looked at her.

McKale wasn't intimidated by Falene—at least she never expressed it. I guess she was just confident in herself and her hold on me. Why wouldn't she be? I had tunnel vision. McKale was everything.

In spite of my melancholy, or maybe because of it, I decided to make my dinner a celebration of three things. First, passing the halfway mark of my walk. Second, returning to my walk. And third, surviving my tumor.

I ordered the same meal I had the night I dined at Ruth's Chris with McKale: sweet potato casserole with pecans, asparagus with Hollandaise sauce, and the Cowboy Ribeye steak. In keeping with my celebration, I complemented my meal with a small glass of red wine, and, alone, made a symbolic toast to the journey. "To Key West," I said. I sounded pathetic. There were better things to toast. I raised my glass again. "To McKale."

I didn't rush, giving myself time to digest both my food and the significance of the moment. When I'd finished eating, I ordered a decaf coffee to go, then went back up to my room. Again, I was surprisingly exhausted.

Outside my window, the arch was lit by spotlights.

I ran my bath and lay back in it, closing my eyes and letting my body soak. I wondered when I'd have that luxury again. Not soon, I wagered. I told myself it was just as well. I was getting soft, and it was time to get back to the road.

CHAPTER

Fifteen

I have been taken in by a Pentecostal
pastor who speaks openly of miracles
and the "fruits of the spirit." I don't
know if there are fewer miracles today
or if, in times past, all unexplained
phenomena was just ascribed to divine
providence. It seems today that we see
less spiritual fruit than religious nuts.

Alan Christoffersen's diary

I forgot to request a wake-up call and woke after ten, which upset me, as I had planned on getting an early start. I quickly dressed, then, taking my pack, went downstairs for breakfast. For the sake of time I opted for the buffet, which was quite good, and checked out of the hotel. Then, without ceremony, I resumed my walk.

I don't think the Gateway Arch can be fully appreciated until one stands at its base and looks up. In spite of my late start, I walked across the street to the monument. I was tempted to take the tour, but it really wasn't an option. There was a security checkpoint at the monument's entrance, and I had my backpack, which they wouldn't allow inside—especially since I was still carrying the gun my father had given me after I was mugged outside of Spokane.

There was no easy way out of the city and, after an hour of trying to navigate a labyrinth of roads and highways, passing through industrial areas of questionable safety, I finally just hailed a cab, which I took twelve miles to the Lindbergh Boulevard freeway exit. I got out near a HoneyBaked Ham store and began walking toward Highway 61.

I was in a suburban part of St. Louis County and the

landscape was green and pretty. I crossed the Meramec River before reaching the town of Arnold, introduced by a sign that read:

ARNOLD

"A Small Town with a Big Heart"

It could just as well have read, *Another small town with an unoriginal slogan*, as I had seen the exact claim at least a dozen times before on my walk. The town was unremarkable in appearance as well, consisting of weather-worn aluminum-sided buildings housing used car dealerships, thrift stores, and hardware shops—the kind of commerce that springs up naturally in small towns, the way willows grow near slow-moving streams.

Around two o'clock, just shy of ten miles into the day's walk, I reached Bob's Drive-In, which boasted the "Best Burger in Town." The claim was probably more than hyperbole, as I hadn't seen another hamburger place since I entered Arnold. Of course, claiming the title by default would also make them the "Worst Burger in Town," but it rarely pays to advertise our faults. Sometimes, but rarely.

Bob's was a true takeout—there was no inside dining—and I stood in front of the boxy diner studying Bob's sizable menu, which was hand-painted on a board hanging over three sliding-glass windows. I walked up to the middle window and rang a bell for service. A brunette woman in her mid-thirties slid open the window.

"What can I get you?"

I took a step forward. "I'll have a Pepsi and your Arnold Burger." I looked back up at the sign. "What's fried okra?"

"It's just okra. Fried."

I smiled at her description. "What's okra?"

She looked at me in disbelief. "It's a vegetable. Some people call it gumbo."

"Like shrimp gumbo?"

"Shrimp gumbo has okra in it," she said. "It's good. You've really never had fried okra?"

"It's new to me."

"You're not from around here, are you?"

"I'm from the northwest."

"That explains things. What brings you to Arnold?"

"I'm just passing through. I'm walking across America."

Her eyes widened. "Shut the door! What city did you start in?"

"Seattle."

"Seattle! Wow. That is so cool. Tell you what, that Pepsi's on me. Are you gonna try the okra?"

"Of course," I said.

"Great. I'll put your order in." She walked away from the window and I heard her calling out my order to someone in back. A moment later she returned with my drink.

"Here's your Pepsi."

"Thank you."

"What's your name?" she asked.

"Alan," I said.

"Nice to meet you, Alan," she said. "I'm Lori."

"Pleasure," I said. "You're from Arnold?"

"No. I live four miles south of here in Barnhart. I'm telling you, you coming through here is the most exciting thing that's happened in Arnold this month."

Hearing this made me a little sad for the people of Arnold.

A bell rang and Lori said, "There's your order. I'll be right back." She returned with a tray holding a hamburger wrapped in yellow waxed paper and a paper sack with my okra, which was lightly fried, the interior a greenish-yellow pod. She rang up my bill. "That'll be six forty-nine."

I took out my wallet and paid her. "Thank you." I carried my food over to one of the little tables. The burger and Pepsi were good. The okra I could pass on. I finished eating my burger, then said goodbye to Lori.

"What did you think of the okra?" she asked.

"I'm glad I tried it," I said, finishing the thought in my head, *so I know not to order it again.*

"Glad you enjoyed it," she said happily. "Can I refill your cup?"

"Actually, could you just put some ice and water in it?"

"Of course. You can just toss that, I'll get you a new cup." She returned a minute later with my water.

"Thank you," I said. "Have a great day."

"You too. Good luck on your walk."

I shrugged on my pack and started off again.

Over the next several miles the landscape grew more rural, and homes and buildings became farther apart. An hour from Arnold, I reached Barnhart, the hometown of Lori at Bob's Drive-In.

Two hours later the landscape changed to broad, green cornfields. It was already getting dark, and I began looking for a place to spend the night. In trying to prove to myself that I was fully recovered, I had done the opposite. My head was aching and I felt too exhausted to erect my tent, but the sky was threatening, so I started looking for a structure I could sleep under. After wandering a while I came to a church with a sign that read:

Connection Worship
Experience Pentecost

On the side of the church was an open, three-walled shed. I walked up a wide, gravel drive to the building and knocked on the door to the church. A minute later a corpulent, red-faced man, with curly, receding hair and a broad smile, welcomed me.

"Good evening. What can I do for you, my friend?"

"I'm just passing through town. I was wondering if I could sleep in your shed over there."

"I'm afraid that wouldn't be very comfortable. But you can sleep inside. We have an extra bedroom."

"I really don't want to be any trouble," I said.

"I live for trouble," the man said wryly. "Come in, come in." He stepped back from the door and motioned me inside. "You can set your pack there on the floor. Can I get you a hot tea and some banana nut bread? One of our congregation brought some over this afternoon."

"Really, I don't want to be a burden."

"What burden?" he said. "I was just about to make myself a cup of tea. I would enjoy the company."

"I would love some," I said.

He led me down a long, dark hall to a small, boxy kitchen with a glass-topped table for four. "Have a seat. I've got a fruits-of-the-forest blend herbal tea that's quite nice. And there's no caffeine to keep you up."

"Thank you," I said.

He turned a flame on beneath the kettle, then dropped four slices of banana nut bread into the toaster. He joined me at the table, putting out his hand. "I'm Pastor Tim."

"Alan Christoffersen," I said.

"Pleased to know you, Brother Christoffersen. Good name you have there."

"How's that?"

"Christ-offers-son. Not theologically correct, I suppose, but close enough. Could be 'God offers Son,' or 'Christ, the offered Son,' but any name with Christ in it is a blessing." The toast popped up. "Would you like yours with butter?"

"Yes, please."

He buttered the bread and returned to the table. Almost the instant he sat down, the kettle began whistling and he popped back up. He poured the steaming water into a teacup. "Honey or sugar?"

"Honey," I said.

He brought the tea and honey over to the table. "Be careful, it's a bit hot."

I squeezed some honey into the cup, then tried a sip.

"I can get you some ice if it's too hot," he said.

"It's fine," I said. "It tastes good."

"Good. Good." He took a bite of bread. "Sister Balfe makes a mean banana bread loaf."

I smiled at his choice of words. I took two Tylenol from my front pocket and took them with my tea.

"Headache?" he asked.

I nodded, then took another sip of tea. "Your sign out front says to experience Pentecost. What does that mean?"

"Are you familiar with the Bible?"

"Some."

"In the New Testament we read that following the resurrection of Christ, the spirit was poured down upon the Apostles during the Feast of Pentecost. The celebration had brought large crowds of people to Jerusalem, and the Apostles were given the gift of tongues and taught the people about Christ in their native languages.

"The event was prophesied by the prophet Joel, 'And it shall come to pass in the last days, saith God, I will pour out of my Spirit upon all flesh: and your sons and your daughters shall prophesy, and your young men shall see visions, and your old men shall dream dreams.' In the Pentecostal faith we welcome such gifts."

"People really speak in foreign languages?"

"Yes, they do. The Bible tells us that God's the same today as He was yesterday. Why would the gifts change?"

"I guess you don't hear about them much."

"No, you don't. Gifts of the spirit require faith. People today don't want the gifts. They don't want the mystical, they want something they can quantify. They want science. If someone today saw a burning bush like Moses did, they'd douse it with a fire extinguisher." He smiled. "The gifts of the Spirit are the fruit of the tree of faith. The gift of tongues, healings and miracles are the blessings of faith. We live in an age of unbelief, but I promise you, miracles still abound. Are you going to still be in town on Sunday?"

I shook my head. "No. Sorry."

"Shame. I think you'd enjoy our meeting. If you ever find your way back here, I invite you to join us."

"Thank you. I will." I wasn't just being polite. His explanation of spiritual gifts made me curious to see them.

When we'd finished our tea and bread, I retrieved my pack and the pastor took me to a bedroom near the front entrance, a small room painted eggshell white with a simple twin bed without a headboard.

"Sorry it's not the Ritz, but it's definitely a notch up from the shed you requested."

"It's great. Thank you."

"The bathroom's at the end of the hall. If you need anything, just holler. My wife's in Fort Wayne visiting her sister, so you don't have to worry about running into anyone."

"Thank you for everything," I said. "Good night."

"Night, my friend." He shut my door and I listened to his footsteps disappear down the hall.

I was still hungry, so I ate an apple, a Pop-Tart, nuts and some jerky. Then I turned down the bed, undressed and turned off the lights. As I lay in bed, I thought about what the pastor had said about miracles. Did they still happen today? Had they ever? I hadn't seen miracles in my life, but perhaps it was my own fault. I certainly wasn't looking or asking for them.

No, that's not true. I had asked for miracles before. I had prayed as sincerely as a man could for McKale's life to be spared.

I rolled over and went to sleep.

CHAPTER

Sixteen

Everyone has suffered
more than you know.

Alan Christoffersen's diary

The next morning I lay in bed taking stock of myself. My body was sore all over from my first full day back walking, but especially my feet, ankles and calves. In spite of my workouts in Pasadena, I felt as if I'd pushed too hard. Thankfully my headache was gone. My head itched a little along the line of my incision and I ran a finger down the scar. Even though my hair had grown long enough to partially conceal it, the skin around it was still raised and numb.

There was a light knock at my door.

"Come in," I said.

The door opened just enough for the pastor to look in. "Sorry to wake you."

"I was just lying here," I said.

"I'm making breakfast. How do you like your eggs?"

"I'm not picky. However the spirit moves you."

He laughed. "All right, divinely inspired eggs. I'm still making biscuits, so you've got twenty minutes or so. Help yourself to the shower."

After he left, I took some clean clothes and a razor from my pack, then went into the bathroom. A hot shower was an unexpected treat, and I stood beneath the spray for at least ten minutes, shaving in there as well. Then I dressed and went into the kitchen. Pastor Tim already had breakfast on the table.

"Sorry I took so long," I said.

"Not at all. I love a long hot shower." He lifted the lid off a pan, exposing a mound of scrambled eggs and patty sausage. "Help yourself. The sausage has a little kick to it."

I loaded up my plate, then took a couple biscuits. Pastor Tim did the same. As I lifted my fork to eat, he said, "Would you join me in prayer?"

I set down my fork. "Of course."

He bowed his head. "Dear Lord, we are grateful for our many blessings. We are grateful for our meeting and ask a blessing to be upon Alan. Please keep him safe on his journey. We ask Thee to bless this food to our good and us to Thy service, Amen."

"Amen," I said.

"Here's some Tabasco sauce for your eggs if you're so inclined," he said, pushing the bottle toward me. Then he tore open his biscuit, layering sausage and eggs inside. "I love a breakfast sandwich." He looked at me. "After we parted last night, I realized that I hadn't asked you where you're going."

"I'm walking to Key West," I said.

"Ah, beautiful Key West. That's quite a ways. Where did you begin your journey?"

"Seattle."

"My, that is a journey. What's in Key West?"

"It was the farthest distance I could walk from Seattle."

His eyes narrowed with interest. "Then the real question is, what's in Seattle?"

"Memories," I said.

He nodded slowly. "Good ones or bad ones?"

"Both. My wife was killed in a horse-riding accident. I lost her, my home, and my job. I just had to get away."

"I understand," he said. "I lost my first wife. Not in an accident, though. She left me."

"I'm sorry," I said.

"Me too," he replied. "Perhaps that's why I felt so compelled to let you in. We're kindred spirits." He looked at me soulfully. "You know, I've wondered if it's more painful to lose someone you love to death or to lose someone you love because she no longer loves you back."

"I don't know," I said.

"On the surface it seems an easy question. It should be much easier to lose someone who doesn't love you, because why would you want to be with someone who doesn't want you? But rejection's not an easy road. A part of you always wonders what made you so unlovable."

"She must have been crazy," I said. "You're one of the kindest people I've met on my walk."

He smiled sadly. "*You* are being kind. But you're not a woman, and the truth is I'm not much to look at. No one's ever mistaken me for Ryan Goosling."

"I think it's Gosling," I said. "But you're being too hard on yourself."

"No, I'm truthful. I just look at myself in the mirror each morning and remind myself that God looks on the heart." He looked at me. "You're a handsome guy. You probably have women chasing you through every town you walk through."

I ignored his observation. "But you're remarried now?"

He smiled. "Yes. Her name is Melba. Like the toast. We're happy. A virtuous woman is more precious than rubies.

"So, Alan Christ-offers-son, what happens when you reach Key West?"

I shrugged. "Good question. When I left Seattle, I had so far to go that I didn't think about it. I'm not sure that I really believed I would make it."

"Think you'll stay in Key West?"

I shook my head. "No. Maybe I'll go back to Seattle and start my business up again."

"Think you'll ever remarry?"

"I don't know."

"You should. It's not good for man to be alone." A wry grin crossed his face. "We get into all kinds of mischief."

"I'm sure you're right."

"Anyone in the wings?" he asked. "Prospects?"

"Actually, there are two women . . ."

"Ah, that's troubled geometry. The infernal triangle."

I smiled. "One of them used to work for me. The other I met on my walk. I was mugged and beaten and she took care of me."

"A good Samaritan. You can't go wrong with someone like that." Suddenly his expression changed. For a moment he didn't speak, then he said, "Is one of them dark-featured, with long black hair? Ample-chested? Maybe she's Greek. Very pretty, like a model."

I was stunned. "You just described Falene. How did you know that?"

He shook his head slowly. "It's nothing."

"No, it's something," I said. "You just described her. How did you know that?"

He just looked at me, hesitant to answer.

"What aren't you telling me?"

"I just had a vision of her."

"You just had a vision? Right now?"

He nodded.

"What else did you see?"

"She was wearing a wedding dress."

"A wedding dress? Was she with me?"

"She was alone."

For a moment I wasn't sure what to say. "Do you have visions often?"

"No. Occasionally. That's how I knew my wife was cheating." He shook his head. "She ran off with the choir director."

I was quiet a moment, then said, "Never trust a musician."

He looked at me, then burst out laughing. "I suppose you're right." He sighed. "I'm glad you stopped by, Alan."

"Me too," I said. When we'd finished eating, I said, "Let me help you clean up."

"No, you'd better get on your way. You've got a long walk ahead of you."

We stood up from the table. I retrieved my pack from the room, then met Pastor Tim at the front door.

"I have something for you," he said. He held out a small pewter coin engraved with the word FAITH.

"Powerful thing, faith," he said. "All journeys are an act of faith."

I nodded. "My father said I needed faith."

Pastor Tim smiled. "Then there you are."

I took the coin from him and put it in my pocket. "Thanks."

"And about the vision. Don't think about it too much. Just have faith that God's at the wheel."

I wasn't sure how to take that. I finally just said, "Thank you for everything."

"My pleasure. God be with you on your journey, Brother Christoffersen."

"And on yours," I replied.

"Well said," he replied. "Well said."

I put on my hat and set out again, grateful for the man's kindness.

Again, I had gotten a late start, but this time I was glad for it, as I felt rested. In spite of the pastor's admonition, I couldn't stop thinking about his vision. Falene in a wedding dress? This had to be a sign, didn't it?

CHAPTER

Seventeen

People can become so blinded by their
own perceived victimhood that they
make victims of everyone around them.

Alan Christoffersen's diary

The next town I walked through was called Pevely, where I came across a cultural relic of the American past—a drive-in theater. I couldn't tell if it still functioned as a drive-in, but I doubted it. The screen was still there, but it looked a bit worn and tall weeds grew up from myriad cracks in the asphalt. The sign out front read:

Pevely Flea Market

I've always had a special place in my heart for drive-in theaters. I have fond childhood memories of lying between my parents in the back of our green, wood-paneled Dodge station wagon watching a Disney movie. I once wrote an essay on drive-in theaters in a high school English class.

You probably don't realize that someone actually holds a patent on the drive-in theater. The original drive-in was created by a Camden, New Jersey, man named Richard Hollingshead. His idea was to create a "family experience," a solution to finding a babysitter. "Now it doesn't matter how much the baby cries," the first advertisement for his theater read. I suppose Hollingshead failed to realize that parents actually went out to get *away* from the crying baby. Not that it mattered. He still hit the bull's-eye, just on a different target. The theater became a make-out haven for youth who knew they *wouldn't* run into their parents.

Drive-in theaters always reminded me of what might be the most bizarre thing I did as a teenager. One mid-summer afternoon McKale, one of her cousins and I were just sitting around the house bored when McKale said, "We should go see a drive-in movie tonight."

The closest drive-in was a one-screen theater located in the nearby town of Monrovia. The movie playing that night was *Braveheart*, an Academy Award winning movie about Scottish rebel William Wallace, played by actor Mel Gibson.

That's when a bizarre idea struck me. "I've got a better idea," I said.

The three of us took some of my father's old clothes, stuffed them with newspapers and rags, and then safety-pinned them together, making a life-sized dummy. We made its head out of a garbage sack stuffed with wadded-up newspaper. McKale dubbed our creation "Mr. Vertigo" in homage to the Hitchcock movie starring Jimmy Stewart and Kim Novak.

Carrying our dummy and a ball of kite string, we walked along the wooden fence at the back of the theater until we found a hole someone had dug beneath it, and snuck inside. This is the crazy part. Slinging the dummy over my shoulder, I climbed up the back of the screen about a hundred feet to the very top.

The prank seemed like a much better idea from the ground, as shimmying seven stories up the rusted metal railing was terrifying—especially when I startled a flock of nesting starlings who weren't pleased to encounter a human in their neighborhood.

When I reached the top of the screen, I clung for my life with one hand and pulled the dummy from my back with the other, laying him across the horizontal beam that ran the length of the screen. I tied the end of our ball of string to the dummy and threw it down over the front of the screen to McKale and her friend, then shimmied back down.

When I reached the ground, McKale yanked the string. To our dismay, the string snapped six feet above us, dangling just out of reach. Unwilling to abandon our prank, I climbed the screen again, retied the string to the dummy and climbed back down. This time I carefully tugged the string until Mr. Vertigo fell over the front of the screen, hurtling headlong to his death. I think the movie viewers appreciated our prank, judging by the honking horns and screams.

McKale spotted a group of people running toward our dummy from the projection house so we ran too, leaving Mr. Vertigo behind to answer for our crimes.

Two evenings later my dad called me in to his den. "Did you drop a dummy from the top of the Monrovia Drive-in Theater?"

It was pointless denying my involvement in the affair, as the very fact that he asked meant he somehow already knew. Though I was afraid of getting in trouble, I was more curious as to how he'd found out. "Yes, sir."

"How did you get the dummy up there?"

"I carried it up."

"You climbed to the top of the screen?"

"Yes, sir." I left out the part about doing it twice.

"That sounds dangerous."

"I know."

"Don't do it again. I don't want you hurting yourself."

"Yes, sir. How did you know?"

"I got a call from the theater. There was a dry cleaner's slip in the pants pocket. Next time ask before taking my clothes. I still wore those pants."

"Sorry," I said.

He went back to his paper. "You can go." As I was walking out, he said, "Al."

"Yes, sir?"

"Did it look real? Like someone falling?"

"I think so."

He nodded. "That's pretty funny. I would have liked to have seen it."

He never brought the incident up again. I think I liked him more after that.

✶

Two miles from Pevely was the town of Herculaneum, named after the ancient Roman twin city of Pompeii. It was also the city where the fictional character Richie Walters in the musical *A Chorus Line* was born.

An hour later I passed through a town called Festus. (The name made me think of the singing deputy of *Gunsmoke*. I used to watch the reruns with my father.) Festus had a population of 11,643—double that of Pevely—evidenced by the town's largest edifice: a Walmart.

> As Americans stopped building town squares
> and piazzas, Walmarts took their place.
>
> —Alan Christoffersen's diary

I was glad to see a Walmart as I was running low on supplies. I bought fruit, a bag of mini bell peppers, a half dozen energy bars, a can of salted peanuts, a dozen flour tortillas, a package of sliced turkey, a bottle of Tabasco sauce, two large bags of beef jerky, Pop-Tarts, four cans of chili, and batteries for my flashlight.

For lunch I bought a V8 juice and a foot-long sandwich from the deli section. As I waited at the register, a large, unkempt woman stepped in line behind me, setting an industrial-sized bag of cheese puffs and a six-pack of beer on the conveyor belt.

The clerk was handing me my change when the woman suddenly clutched her chest and groaned out. "Oh, I'm having a heart attack. Call 911!"

The young woman behind the counter just stood there, frozen, her eyes wide with panic.

"Call 911!" I said. This time the young woman grabbed her phone and dialed. I helped the gasping woman to the floor in the middle of the checkout aisle. "How do you feel?" I asked.

"My chest," she wheezed. "It feels like an elephant's sitting on it. I can't breathe!"

"Try to stay calm," I said. "Help will be here soon." I looked back up at the clerk. "Did you call 911?"

"They're on their way."

"Help me over to the bench," the woman said.

"No," I said. "I think you should just stay here."

"No," she insisted. "The bench." To my surprise, she climbed to her feet, then waddled to a bench about twenty feet away from the aisle. I followed her, unsure of what to do. Fortunately it was only a few minutes before we heard the wail of sirens. Just seconds later, two paramedics rushed into the store carrying bags of gear. I stood and waved them over.

As the lead paramedic neared, I saw his expression change. He looked at the woman with unmistakable annoyance. When he got to her side, he knelt down and took her hand, placing a pulse oximeter on the end of her index finger. Then he glanced back at his partner.

"Ninety-seven," he said.

His partner handed him a blood pressure cuff. The paramedic said, "All right, Rosie. You know the drill."

The woman pulled up her sleeve and the young man strapped the cuff on.

"How am I, Doctor?" she asked.

"I'm not a doctor," he said. "Hypertensive. Nothing unusual." He turned back to his partner. "One fifty-eight over ninety-three."

As quickly as he had arrived, the paramedic unfastened the cuff and began returning his gear to its bag. His partner just stood there, his arms folded at his chest, his expression dour.

I watched the incident unfold with confusion. "How is she?"

The paramedic looked at me with a dull expression. "She's fine," he said. "She's diabetic and has mild hypertension, but other than that, she's fine."

I glanced over at the woman, then back. "Really? But she . . ."

"Rosie's *always* fine."

"What do you mean, *always*?"

He stood up with his bag, turning away from the woman. "Rosie here is what we call a 'frequent flier.' She fakes heart attacks, then tells people to call 911."

I looked at the woman, who seemed oblivious to our talking about her, then back at the paramedic. "Why would she do that?"

"Because she *can*," he said sharply. "It's a rush for her. She gets a lot of attention and feels powerful that we all have to come running. And every time we do, it costs the taxpayers five grand."

"You're kidding me."

"I wish I were."

"Can't you do something about it?"

His eyebrows rose. "Like what? You tell me. Even if we knew it was her, if we didn't respond, some ambulance chasing lawyer would sue the city. The worst part is, last week while we were playing her game, a man on the other side of town had a real heart attack. Some bystanders kept him alive for nineteen minutes, four minutes short of what it took us to get to him."

"You're telling me that she killed him."

"We can't say that for sure, but he sure as hell would have had a better chance of living if we'd been there."

I turned back and looked at the woman with disgust. "Did you know that? This game you play cost a man his life."

She scowled at me. "You think just because I'm poor I'm not entitled to the same care everyone else is?"

"This has nothing to do with rich or poor," I said angrily. "It has to do with need."

"It has to do with crazy," the other paramedic said.

"I have problems," the woman said.

"Clearly," I replied. "You're an awful person."

She just stared at me, her mouth gaping like a fish on land. I went back and got my groceries, then left the store.

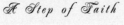

Drama aside, the rest of the afternoon was decent walking as Festus gave way to more rural landscape. Physically, I felt better than I had the day before, giving me hope that perhaps the worst was over. As night fell, I reached the Good News Church, a golf course, and Mary's Market, where I stopped for hot coffee. I pitched my tent and camped in a gully on the side of the road.

Every time I thought about that woman at Walmart, I wanted to slap her.

CHAPTER

Eighteen

We cannot enslave others without
enslaving a part of ourselves.

Alan Christoffersen's diary

I had set up my tent on a slight incline and woke the next morning with a crick in my neck, which I tried to release by cracking it, but it didn't help much.

I walked back to Mary's Market and bought some yogurt, coffee, and a giant homemade blueberry muffin. I sat on the curb outside the store and ate my breakfast, then set out for the day.

The morning sky was clear and brilliant blue, and I walked on a smooth road of light-colored asphalt. I was on the "Great River Road" which, technically, was still U.S. 61 South.

Two and a half hours later I reached the tiny town of Bloomsdale, and stopped at the side of the road at the not-so-cleverly named Roadside Park. I ate an early lunch of tortillas stuffed with sliced turkey, bell peppers and hot sauce, then laid my map out over a picnic table. Twelve miles ahead was Ste. Genevieve. I packed away my food and pressed ahead, eager to reach the historic town before nightfall.

✳

Ste. Genevieve, named for the patron saint of Paris, was founded in 1735, more than a quarter-century before

America declared its independence. I passed through a neighborhood of small, nondescript houses, built close together, to the town's historical district, which was quaint and pleasing.

There were several bed and breakfasts in the center of town, but one in particular caught my eye:

The Southern Hotel
An Historic Bed & Breakfast Inn
Innkeepers Mike and Cathy Hankins

I rang the buzzer and a pleasant looking woman wearing an apron opened the door.

"Good evening, may I help you?"

"Do you have any vacancies?"

"Yes we do," she said, pulling the door open. "Come in and I'll show you what we have available."

I stepped inside. The foyer was wood-paneled and adorned with beautiful paintings, shadow boxes, and wall hangings, which included several patchwork quilts.

"Come into the parlor," she said.

I followed her through a set of saloon doors into the parlor and carefully set my pack down.

"We just had these doors put in," the woman said. "These front rooms were used as a saloon until prohibition time, so we thought it would be a nice nod to the history of the place."

The parlor had a two-person settee and several wingback chairs upholstered in red velvet. There was a bookcase full of old-time parlor games and a large fireplace with a walnut mantel.

"What is your name?" she asked, holding up a pen.

"Alan Christoffersen."

"Alan," she repeated. "My name is Cathy. When we're done, you can park your car on the side of the house."

"I don't have a car."

She looked at me quizzically. "Oh? How did you get here?"

"I walked."

"From where?"

I was more tired than talkative so I just said, "St. Louis."

She still looked impressed. "That's a long way. You must be tired. Let's get you a room. We have three rooms available for tonight, and they're all the same price. Would you like to see them before checking in?"

"I'm sure one of them will be fine," I said.

She nodded. "I think you'll be pleased."

I handed her my credit card and she ran it through a machine, then handed it back to me. "Let me tell you a little about the house." She pointed to a framed picture above the fireplace mantel. "That's the Valle family, the home's original owners. They had seven children and fifteen slaves."

"Slaves?"

"Yes, the home is more than two hundred years old," she said. "That nonsense was still going on. The slaves slept on the top floor. Actually, in one of the rooms we have available.

"If you'll follow me, I'll show you the dining room." She led me across the parlor to the dining area. "Breakfast is served at eight o'clock and nine o'clock. We've won awards for our food, so come prepared to eat."

"That won't be a problem," I said.

Cathy led me to the staircase and we walked all the

way to the top floor. At the top of the stairs I noticed another steep stairway leading up to a hatch door in the ceiling.

"Is that the attic?"

"No, that's the belvedere," she replied. "It's a rooftop structure designed to give you a view. It comes from an Italian word meaning good view—at least that's what Mike told me. You're welcome to go up, but it's hotter than heck. This time of year we just call it the sauna."

"I'd like to see it," I said.

Cathy frowned a little. "I was afraid you would."

I followed her up the creaking stairs to the trap door, which she pushed open, and light and heat flooded down on us. She was right about the "sauna." I followed her through the hatch and climbed up into a small room, which was hot and humid enough that it was difficult to breathe. The octagon-shaped structure had windows on all eight sides giving an unobstructed, 360-degree view of the city.

Cathy turned to me. She was panting a little and per-spiration beaded on her face and neck. "During the Civil War, the Union Army occupied the building. This was their lookout. As you can see, they could keep an eye on the entire town from up here."

The heat prohibited us from spending much time up there, and my underarms and back were damp with sweat when I climbed back down to the cooler floor below. Cathy led me into a room near the stairway.

"This is the Quilt Room," she said. "It's one of the rooms where the slaves were kept."

"How do you know?"

"It was pretty standard to keep slaves in the attic at the time. They slept up here during the winter when heat would rise from the fireplaces, and they stayed downstairs in the cellar during the hot summers. But there's other evidence." She pointed across the room to a ball-and-claw-foot tub. "If you look under the tub, you can see the metal ring that slaves were chained to at night to keep them from escaping."

I walked over to the tub and leaned over it. "Over here?"

"You can see it better from the floor. You'll have to get down on all fours."

I got down on my knees and looked underneath. Six inches from the wall was a large, rusted metal ring secured to the floor. "They chained people to this?"

"Unfortunately."

The idea of it sickened me. I didn't want to stay in the room.

"As I said before, the original owners had fifteen slaves. Two of their slaves were assigned just to chopping wood and keeping all the fireplaces going. There was also a tale that they owned a very large slave who was fathered out to other slaveholders in the area. Some said the slave was buried in the home's cellar after he died. A few years back, Mike let an archeologist dig in there for his bones, but he didn't find anything."

We walked through two other rooms. I chose the third, the "Buttons and Bows" room, which featured a shadow-box button collection from 1720, a working fireplace, two tubs, and a black and white wedding photograph accompanied by the bride's actual veil. The room was wallpapered with golden fleur-de-lis over a rose-colored background. The bed was unlike any I'd seen before: polished rosewood with four posts and a canopy extending over just half the bed.

"This kind of bed's called a half tester," she said. "It was made in 1775. They're hard to find." Cathy pointed to the two bathtubs, standing side by side in the corner of the room. "Those are made of cast iron and porcelain, the combination really keeps the heat in. Whenever we have couples staying in this room, we hear that the woman gets the longer tub and the man gets stuck with the shorter one." She smiled at me. "But you're lucky—you won't have that problem."

I let the comment roll off of me. I followed her back downstairs, retrieved my pack, then said goodnight and went back up to the room. I filled up both of the tubs, one for soaking my dirty socks and underwear and the other for me. After a long, relaxing bath I rinsed out my laundry and hung it over the radiator, which wasn't on but was still the best surface I could find for laying out my things. I climbed into bed and went to sleep.

The next morning I slept until seven-thirty. My headache was back, a dull ache near my incision. I collected my washing, which, fortunately, was dry, dressed and packed, then, taking my backpack with me, went downstairs for breakfast. There were two couples in the room, but neither of them acknowledged my entrance.

Cathy greeted me as I entered the dining room. "How did you sleep, Alan?"

"Well, thank you."

"You can sit wherever you like," she said.

I chose a small, round table away from the other guests. Across the room from me, a tall, walnut-cased grandfather clock chimed the hour.

"I think you'll enjoy this morning's breakfast," Cathy said. "It's our guests' favorite: crustless quiche with sausage, and our special cream cheese blackberry muffins."

"It sounds delicious," I said.

She smiled. "Trust me, it is."

A few minutes later she returned with my plate, then left me alone to eat. I ate slowly, not in a particular hurry to get back on the road. In spite of a good night's rest, I still felt tired. A half hour later, Cathy emerged from the kitchen.

"How is everything?" she asked.

"As good as you said it would be."

She smiled. "Well, I didn't mean to boast."

"You should," I said. "How's business?"

"Pretty good. We're not going to be buying the St. Louis Cardinals anytime soon, but we enjoy what we're doing."

"That's better than owning the Cardinals," I said.

"I'll have to take your word for that."

"My wife would really like it here," I said.

"Then you'll just have to bring her next time," she said. "Excuse me. I need to check on the oven." She walked back to the kitchen, but returned a few minutes later with a basket of hot muffins.

"Here you go, hot out of the oven."

I took one. "How do you like living in Ste. Genevieve?"

"I love it here. It has so much history and charm. Ste. Genevieve is a very old town. In fact, it's older than our country. It was settled mostly by French-Canadians, and a lot has been done to preserve the original French-colonial style. Did you see the Old Brick House?"

I shook my head.

"It's just around the corner. It's a restaurant now, but it's famous for being the first brick building west of the Mississippi."

"Did you grow up here?" I asked.

"No. I actually came to stay at the Southern Hotel just a few years after Mike's first wife Barbara passed. I brought my granddaughter for a special trip, and the second Mike opened the front door, I was smitten. It took him a little longer to come around, but when he did, he just about ran me over."

"Mike owned the hotel before he met you?"

"Yes. He and Barbara were just passing through town. They were at the candle shop across the street when they noticed a big FOR SALE sign in front of the hotel. In less than a week they were the owners. It took nine months and more than forty people to restore it, but the place has been receiving guests ever since."

"How long have you and Mike been married?"

She counted on her fingers. "Five years this Thanksgiving."

"What's it like being married to a widower?"

"That's an interesting question," she said. "I suppose it's like any marriage." She suddenly grinned. "Except I don't hit him if he calls me by another woman's name."

"Does he ever do that?"

"Call me Barbara? Every now and then. Usually when he's in a hurry. Old habits die hard."

"Does it bother you?"

She thought for a moment, then said, "No, not really. In a way it's a compliment. He loved his first wife dearly. And even though I never met her, I feel a connection to her that I can't quite explain. I think we would have been good friends." She shook her head. "That probably sounds strange."

I thought of McKale and Falene. "No," I said. "It's actually quite beautiful."

She smiled. "Thank you."

I finished my muffin, then said, "I guess I've delayed the inevitable long enough, I better get going." I stood up from the table and lifted my pack. "Breakfast was terrific. Actually, everything was. Thank you."

"Don't mention it. Stop by again sometime. And next time, bring your wife."

"That would be nice," I said.

As I walked toward the door, Cathy said, "Oh, don't forget to sign the quilt." She pointed to a stitched quilt mounted to the wall. "We have all our guests sign it." She handed me a marker.

I signed my name, then walked out of the house. McKale definitely would have loved this place.

✦

Following Cathy's directions, I left Ste. Genevieve on a different road from the one I came in on. Before I left the city, I passed a shop with a sign in its window advertising "KEY WEST." I walked up to read what it had to say. Key West turned out to be the name of a local "island" band.

The route Cathy gave me bypassed the residential areas, taking me directly back to 61 South. The longer I walked, the more I wished I had stayed another day in Ste. Genevieve. In addition to feeling crummy, I had to deal with the weather. The sky was dark and gray, and a little before noon it began raining hard enough that water ran off the brim of my hat. I was walking on a narrow shoulder of highway, and the fast traffic on slick roads not only put my life in peril, but guaranteed that I was frequently splashed by passing vehicles. The air was muggy, thick with humidity and the loud sound of bugs and birds distressed by the rain.

Thankfully, the rain and my headache lightened some by late afternoon as I entered the town of Brewer. It was another small, rural town, and what struck me as most peculiar about the place was that it had the biggest front lawns I'd ever seen. *These folks don't need tractor mowers,* I thought, *they need combines.*

Two miles later I reached Perryville, the largest town of the day with a population of more than 8,000. I walked into town wet, tired and shivering. I took a room at the first hotel I found, a Budget Inn. I took off my wet clothes, showered, then ate dinner at a nearby Hardee's.

✦

The sky cleared during the night. The road still wasn't much for walking, narrow and grated with a severe rumble strip, and I stumbled more than once. Still, it wasn't raining and I was grateful for that. And the scenery was bucolic. I passed beautiful red barns, and long, expertly cultivated rows of crops, marked and numbered with agricultural signs from the seed vendors for commercial demonstration.

A little over six miles into the day I reached my first town, Longtown, with a population of just 102. For such a small town it had an impressive church—Zion Lutheran— a large structure with pointed-arch windows and a tall white steeple. In addition to the church, Longtown also boasted an abnormally large number of plastic deer in its residents' front yards, which are only slightly weirder than plastic pink flamingos.

That afternoon I saw one other peculiar thing—a herd of cows gathered around a small bonfire. There were no humans in sight and I wasn't sure what to make of it. I was fairly certain that the cows hadn't started the fire, so I just kept on walking.

That evening I set up my tent in a grove of trees near a picturesque farm with three silos.

CHAPTER

Nineteen

I have so often compared my life to a
whirlwind that I should not be surprised
to find myself facing a real one.

Alan Christoffersen's diary

The next morning I woke to the sound of howling wind and rain pelting my tent. *Another day in paradise*, I thought. My map showed that I was still about eight miles from the nearest town, so I ate breakfast in my tent, then lay back, waiting for the rain to weaken. After an hour the weather still hadn't relented, so I gave up and started off for the day.

My pace was slowed by the storm, and by the time I reached the town of Fruitland, I was cold and drenched. I stopped at a gas mart called Casey's for supplies, then walked to the nearby Jer's Restaurant for lunch.

A broad, surly-looking woman glanced up from the counter. "You're all wet," she said.

I wasn't sure if she was annoyed that I was dripping on her floor or if she just had a penchant for stating the obvious. "I've heard that before," I said.

She just glared at me.

After a moment I said, "It's raining."

"It's going to get worse," she said. "We've got a severe weather warning. Maybe even tornadoes."

"Tornadoes?"

She nodded.

Outside of *The Wizard of Oz* and the Weather Channel,

I had never seen a tornado. It was one experience I didn't care if I missed. "Is there anyplace in town to stay?"

"Closest hotel is a couple miles ahead in Jackson."

I took off my hat and scratched my head. "A couple of miles, huh?"

"You want something to eat?" she asked sternly.

"Yes."

"Pick a table," she said.

I looked around. The restaurant was empty except for a truck driver in a corner booth who was nursing a cola and playing a video game on his cell phone.

I sat down at a booth on the opposite side of the diner, then lay my pack on the chair next to me and put my hat on top of it. When Miss Congeniality returned, I ordered fried chicken with mashed potatoes and gravy.

In spite of the woman's warning of worsening weather, I ate slowly, hoping the rain might ease up a little. As predicted, it got worse. I ordered a piece of peach pie to buy me more time in the shelter, then, finally accepting my inevitable drenching, paid my bill, put on my hat and walked out into the storm, hoping for better hospitality from the next town. Or the tornado.

Although Jackson was just two miles from Fruitland, in weather conditions like these, it seemed much farther. At one point my hat blew off and I chased it for several minutes.

As I neared the town, the rain came down harder. The sky had turned black, lit with what seemed an increasing frequency of lightning strikes—sometimes even simultaneous with the thunder. It occurred to me that even though I hadn't seen a funnel cloud, this was what tornado weather looked like on the Weather Channel.

As I crossed the Jackson city line, the rain suddenly

turned to hail, bouncing off me and the street like water on a hot griddle. Some of the hail was nearly golf-ball-sized and it hurt. Lifting my pack over my head, I made a fifty-yard dash for cover beneath a highway overpass.

When I reached the shelter of the bridge, my heart was pounding heavily from my sprint, and I was as wet as if I had fallen into a lake. Both sides of the overpass were opaque with white sheets of hail. I lay my pack on the ground, then sat down on the curb next to the highway to rest. That's when I heard the sirens.

CHAPTER

Twenty

Is it possible for those on the other side
to intervene on our behalf? Millions of
dollars have been spent on this very hope.

Alan Christoffersen's diary

Tornadoes are rare in both Los Angeles and Seattle—there has never, in the recorded history of either city, been a death caused by one—so, not surprisingly, I had never heard a tornado siren before.

Outside of the bridge there was no shelter in sight. I grabbed my pack and had started to climb up a weeded incline so I could hide under the bottom of the bridge when a navy-blue Nissan Sentra braked below me and honked its horn. The car's passenger window rolled down and I heard a young woman shout, "Get in."

I slid down the embankment, threw my pack in the car's back seat, then opened the front door. The driver was maybe five years younger than me, pretty, with full lips and long, bright red hair, windblown around her face. She had an exotic look, almost feline.

She smiled at me, and her hazel green eyes were bright and kind. I pulled the door shut behind me as she reached forward and turned off the radio, leaving only the sound of my heavy breathing and the wind battering her car.

"Thank you," I said. "I'm drenched."

She smiled at me. "And I'm Paige."

I reached over, taking her hand. "My name is Alan."

"Put your seatbelt on, Alan," she said. "We better get out of here."

As I fastened my belt, she checked her mirror, then pulled out onto the road. As soon as we came out from under the bridge, the sound of the storm exploded. The hail beat against her car like a snare drum.

"That's going to be an insurance claim," she shouted over the noise. She turned to me. "You're crazy being out in this storm. What are you, an extreme hiker? Didn't you hear the sirens?"

"I didn't have a lot of options," I said. "I thought the overpass would be safe."

"No," she said, shaking her head. "You'd probably be safer low to the ground. The higher up you are the more exposed you are to flying debris."

There was a loud thunderclap and she jumped a little.

"Where are we going?" I asked.

"There's a hotel just up ahead. We can stay there until this blows over."

The hail lessened, but not the rain, and the car's wipers whipped violently—though mostly ineffectually—against the downpour. A quarter-mile ahead of us we finally saw the hotel: Drury Inn & Suites. The front of the building was crowded with cars and we parked as close to the entrance as we could.

Paige grabbed a small travel bag from the back seat. "Ready?"

"Let's go."

We simultaneously jumped out of her car. I grabbed my pack from the back seat as she ran for the hotel. She held the door for me as I entered.

Once we were both inside she asked, "Are you okay?"

"Yes," I said, panting. "Just wet."

"You're definitely wet."

"That's okay," I said. "I was born wet."

She laughed.

The hotel's lobby was crowded with the storm's refugees, probably more than a hundred people in all, surrounded by their pets and belongings and huddled together in small clans. I quickly surmised that most of the people weren't hotel guests.

There was a television on in the dining area off the lobby, and a group of men were sitting around it at tables, drinking coffee and, to my surprise, watching football instead of the weather.

Paige and I worked our way through a labyrinth of people to a small corner of the room that no one had yet claimed. I took off my pack and we both sat on the floor. Paige took off her coat, then pulled her long hair back from her face.

"How long were you out there?" she asked.

"A few hours. I walked from the last town."

"No wonder you're so wet," she said. "Where are you from?"

"Seattle. We don't do tornadoes."

She took a brush out of her travel bag and began brushing her hair. "It's Alan, right?"

"Yes. And you're Paige."

"Right. Where are you headed?"

"Key West, Florida."

"All the way from Seattle?"

"That's the plan," I said.

"That's amazing. The farthest I've ever walked at one time was ten miles for a breast cancer fundraiser."

A cardboard box crashed loudly against the window

next to us, and Paige screamed, then laughed at herself. "Sorry, I'm just skittish."

"Where are you from?" I asked.

"I was born in St. Louis. That's where I live now."

"What brings you down here?"

"I'm headed to Memphis to see my grandma. I was hoping to make it by tonight, but it doesn't look like it's going to clear up anytime soon."

"I was planning on walking to Cape Girardeau by evening," I said. "I don't think that's going to happen."

"Not likely," Paige said.

"I wonder if the hotel has any vacancies," I said. "I think I'll check."

I got up and walked to the hotel's front desk. The woman behind the counter was listening to the weather report on the radio, and I could hear a hysterical caller screaming over the sound of the wind that a semi had been blown over. The clerk glanced up at me as I approached. "May I help you?"

"Do you have any rooms?"

"We have two left," she said. "They're both nonsmoking, first-floor rooms with two queen beds."

"I'll take one," I said. I gave her my credit card and driver's license.

"How many room keys do you need?"

I glanced over at Paige, wondering if she trusted me enough to stay with me. "Two," I said.

She slid two plastic cards through her encoder, then handed them to me with my credit card. "There you go. It sounds as if the worst of the storm is over, but if another tornado touches down, the safest place to be will be in the hallway outside your room."

"Thank you," I said.

I walked back over to Paige and lifted my pack. "I've got a room. It's got two beds. You're welcome to hang out with me in there."

"That would be nice. Thank you."

We gathered our things and walked to the room, which was only halfway down the hall off the lobby. The window's curtain was drawn back and rain pelted the glass, coagulating in long streams of runoff.

I threw my hat on the TV cabinet, lay my pack on the floor near the corner, then sat at the foot of the bed and took off my shoes. "How long do these things usually take to pass?"

Paige ran her hand down the length of her bed. "You never know. It'll probably die down in the night." She pulled back the covers and sat down on the bed to take off her shoes.

"You're from St. Louis?" I asked.

"Mostly," she said. "I live there now."

"What do you do?"

"I work for a hospice company."

"Hospice? You help people . . ."

". . . Die," she said. "I know, it sounds sad."

"What's that like?"

"The worst part is that just about the time you start caring for someone you lose them."

"That sounds awful."

"In a way it is. But it's also really rewarding. I can't imagine doing anything else with my life right now."

She lay back on the bed, her long red hair splayed out over her pillow.

"Do you want to watch TV?" I asked.

"Whatever you want," she replied.

"I was asking for you. I'm going to take a shower and get into some dry clothes."

"Oh. Sure," she said.

"Do you need to use the bathroom first?" I asked.

"No. I'm good."

I took some clean clothes out of my pack, then tossed Paige the TV remote and went inside the bathroom. I stayed in the hot water until the bathroom mirror was dripping with condensation. When I came back out, Paige was watching the weather on a local station.

"How is it?" I asked.

"It's looking better." She smiled at me. "You look like you feel a lot better."

"Much," I said. "Any news on the storm?"

"It looks like the tornadoes are gone. It's supposed to clear up by morning."

"I'm glad to hear that."

As I sat down on the bed, she turned off the television. "Tell me about your walk," she said.

"What do you want to know?"

"What states have you been through?"

"I started in Washington, walked through Idaho, Montana, Wyoming, South Dakota, then Iowa, Nebraska, Missouri and here I am. Six more states to go."

"You've walked nonstop?"

"Mostly. I stopped twice, but not by choice. Once was in Spokane when I was mugged."

She blanched. "You were mugged?"

"A gang attacked me. I was stabbed three times."

She stared at me with wide eyes. "Really?"

I raised my eyebrows. "Want to see the scars?"

She nodded, and I lifted my shirt.

She gasped. "Oh, my."

"Another inch higher and I probably wouldn't be here."

"Wow," she said. "I didn't realize Spokane was such a tough place."

I laughed. "It's not. But there's crime everywhere and when you're on the street you're at risk. Gangs, tornadoes . . . redheads."

She smiled. "If it wasn't for a redhead, you might still be under that bridge. Like a troll."

I laughed. "I'm in your debt."

"It's my pleasure. I almost didn't see you. I think I was inspired."

"What do you mean?"

"Every morning when I pray, I ask God to let me help one of His children. As I was approaching the underpass, I had a strong feeling that I needed to slow down. When I looked up, there you were."

"You pray for that every day?" I asked.

"Almost," she said. "It's amazing the opportunities that have come to me since I started doing that. Most of the time it's someone I'm working with in hospice. Sometimes I'll get these flashes of insight into their lives."

"You should be sainted."

"I was thinking the exact same thing," she laughed, holding her hands open around her face. "St. Paige."

I couldn't help but think how cute she looked.

"You said you stopped twice on your walk."

"The second time was in St. Louis. I found out I had a brain tumor after I passed out just outside the city."

"Is that why you have that scar?" she asked, looking at my head.

I nodded. "I was taken to the hospital in St. Louis, then ended up flying home to Pasadena for treatment."

"I thought you said you lived in Seattle."

"I did," I said. "But I left when my wife died."

She frowned. "I'm so sorry. Was she ill?"

"No. She died from complications after a horse-riding accident."

"I'm so sorry," she said again. "Does that have something to do with why you're walking?"

"It's the *reason* I'm walking."

She shook her head slowly. "It's hard losing a loved one."

"You experience it all the time," I said.

"No, I see death," she said softly. "But it's not the same as losing family."

"You've lost someone close?" I asked.

She didn't have to answer. I could see in her eyes that she had.

"I'm sorry," I said. "I shouldn't have asked."

"It's okay," she said. "I want to tell you. I think you might be one of the few people who would understand." She leaned forward on the edge of the bed. "When I was sixteen, my parents decided to take a trip to Denver. I was the oldest, I had a sister who was just a year younger than me and two little brothers. I had cheerleading camp so I couldn't go with them.

"The morning they left, my mother was stressed about leaving me alone and kept nagging me about keeping the house clean while they were gone and 'no parties' and 'no boys' and all the things parents say to irresponsible teenagers. I finally yelled at her and said, 'All right, you're making me crazy. Just get out of here! Just go already!' " Paige frowned. "I'll never forget the hurt in her eyes. She kissed me and told me she loved me, then got up and walked out of my room. I felt so embarrassed for

151

having behaved badly that I didn't even go out to see them off. I just watched from the window." She wiped a tear from her eye. "It was the last time I saw my family.

"My father had just gotten his pilot's license, so he wanted to fly the family to Colorado. On the flight home it was foggy. He got disoriented and crashed into a mountain. Everyone was killed.

"I was taken in by my grandmother, but it was hard. I was a mess. I was grieving and had survivor's guilt. I became really self-destructive. I changed my friends and started drinking. Then I started smoking pot and taking painkillers. I became promiscuous, which made me hate myself even more.

"My grandmother tried to help, but I was too much for her. I told her that she wasn't my mother and to just keep out of my life or I'd move in with my boyfriend. My boyfriend was a worse train wreck than I was. He got me most of my drugs.

"Around that time I developed an eating disorder. I got down to eighty-four pounds. I'm pretty sure that I was trying to kill myself.

"One night I was at a party and one of the boys had brought some heroin. The guy didn't really know anything about the drug, he was just acting cool and handing it out.

"As usual, I was up for anything. My best friend Kylee and I tried it. We took what the kid gave us, which was way too much, especially for our first time. I passed out.

"When I woke, I was in the back of an ambulance throwing up into a bucket. I was so drenched with sweat I thought I had fallen into a swimming pool. I can't describe the pain." She shook her head. "It was . . . horrendous.

"They stabilized me at the hospital. The next morning

I started asking about Kylee. It took a while to find someone who knew anything about her, but I eventually found out. She'd died before the paramedics got there.

"Two days later my grandmother came and picked me up. She was so upset that she didn't say a word to me the whole way home. But as soon as we were inside, she said, 'When are you going to stop this insanity?'

"I said, 'I almost just died.'

"She said, 'Yes, I know.'

"Then I said, 'My *family* died.'

"She said, 'And you think that gives *you* a pass to stop living? My daughter died! And now I'm watching my granddaughter kill herself. Should I just give up on life like you did? Should I be just like you?'

"I told her that I hated her, then I broke down sobbing and ran to my room and locked the door.

"That night I had a very intense dream. I was lying in bed when I suddenly realized that my mother was sitting at the foot of my bed. She looked very sad. I was scared, but I was also so glad to see her. I said 'Mom!' She looked into my eyes and even though she didn't speak, I could hear what she was thinking. She said, 'You are loved, Paige.'

"It took a moment for the message to sink in. I began to cry. I said, 'I don't deserve to be loved.'

"She said, 'Love is not earned. It is a gift from our Father.'

"I said, 'I'm so sorry I didn't go with the family. I should have been with you,' but she said that it wasn't my time. Then I started to apologize for what I'd said to her the morning they left, but before I could finish, she said, 'Paige, you are loved.'

"I just broke down and wept. When I could speak, I

said, 'What do I do?' and she told me to fill my life with love. I said I didn't know how, but she just smiled and said, 'Of course you do. You love me, don't you?'

"When I told her yes, she said, 'Begin there. Begin by treating my mother as if she were me.'

"I asked her if I was dreaming, and she smiled and said, 'Tell Grandma that Babbo says he's still waiting for her answer. And tell her to be patient with the little rose. It's been a tough winter.' Then she said, 'Remember to love my girl,' and she was gone.

"I got up early the next morning. I felt like a new person. I cleaned my room, then I went into the kitchen and made breakfast. Grandma came into the kitchen to see what was going on. She was so surprised. But there was still a lot of tension between us, so she didn't say anything. She went to get her tea and I said, 'Sit down, Grandma. I'll get it.'

"I got her tea and poured it for her. Then I sat down at the table with her. We looked at each other for a moment, then I said, 'I'm very sorry about what I said last night. I didn't mean it.'

"She said, 'Maybe you did.'

"I began to cry. I said, 'No, I think I just hate myself.'

"She stared at me a little longer, then said, 'You came to this last night?'

"I said 'Yes.' We just sat there for a while, then I said, 'I saw Mom last night.'

"She gave me this concerned look. I'm sure she just thought it had something to do with the drugs. I said, 'I don't know what it means, but she said to tell you that Babbo says he's still waiting for an answer.'

"I thought she was going to faint. She turned white as a

sheet, then she began to cry. When she could speak, she said, 'Did she say anything else?'

"I said, 'She said to be patient with the little rose. It's been a tough winter.' "

"Little rose?" I asked.

"I found out later that before I was born, Grandma would pat my mother's belly and call me her little rose."

"And Babbo?"

"Ten years after my grandfather died, my grandmother fell in love again. He was from Italy and his children called him 'Babbo.' It's an Italian term of endearment, like 'Daddy.' She started calling him Babbo too.

"He asked her to marry him. She said she loved him, but she had been single for so long that she wanted to take the weekend to think it over. He joked that he'd come by on Sunday night to collect his 'yes.'

"She made up her mind that she was going to marry him, but he never came by. She called his house the next morning and his son answered. Sunday night he had passed away from a stroke."

Paige paused. I looked down for a moment, then took a deep breath. "What happened next?"

"I changed. I stopped drinking and partying. I got help for my eating disorder and I went with my grandmother back to school to meet with my counselors. I was able to get my grades back up enough to graduate.

"After that, I started working with hospice. Every now and then I'm able to share some of my own experience to help a patient. I have a good life."

"You're headed back to see your grandmother now?" I asked.

"Yes. She's in the final stages of cancer. I guess it's her

turn." She looked up, smiling through her tears. "I don't know what she's going to do with both Grandpa and Babbo up there!"

We both laughed.

※

Later, after we had turned out the lights to go to sleep, Paige asked, "Do you ever feel your wife near you?"

I thought about it. "Sometimes," I said. "Sometimes."

CHAPTER

Twenty-one

The storm has passed. As usual, the
world looks deceivingly safe.

Alan Christoffersen's diary

The storm died in the night. When I woke early the next morning, Paige was already up and getting ready for the day. She came out of the bathroom holding a blow dryer.

"I'm sorry," she said. "Did I wake you?"

"No. I'm an early riser. You look nice."

"Thank you."

"I don't know which is more beautiful, your inside or your outside."

"Are you hitting on me, Alan?"

"No," I said.

"Darn," she said, turning away. "I was hoping you were."

✦

We ate breakfast together in the hotel's dining room. She wrote down her cell phone number and made me promise to contact her when I reached Memphis.

"I'll take you for barbecue at Vergo's Rendezvous," she said.

We said goodbye, hugged, and then, for our own reasons, both headed south.

It was hard to believe that it had only been a week since I had resumed my walk.

In the sunlight, Jackson looked nothing like it had the

night before. I turned left at the city hall building and soon found my way back to 61 South. I reached Cape Girardeau by noon, a decent-sized city with a population of more than 38,000. I ate lunch at the Huddle House, where I ordered breakfast—the Mansion Platter, a rib-eye steak, three fried eggs, hash browns, and biscuits with sausage gravy.

I left the town on Kingshighway, ending up on I-55 to Scott City, where I took exit 89 (a dangerous roundabout for pedestrians) leading back to 61 South. I took the highway for two more miles until I reached the tiny town of Kelso. There were nice homes, but no hotels, so I ended up camping in a grove of trees near an elementary school.

❈

I woke the next day before the sun came up. I ate an orange and a protein bar, then folded up my tent and started walking. It was a beautiful morning and the sun painted the pristine landscape in golden hues. In addition, I had no headache and my muscles weren't sore. It was the nicest walking I'd done since I'd resumed my journey.

The first town I reached was Benton. I stopped to eat breakfast at Mario's Italian Eatery, a prefab building painted dark green with an Italian flag draped over the entrance. It had dozens of hand-painted signs mounted to its exterior, advertising daily specials. I had a breakfast calzone stuffed with mozzarella cheese, eggs and ham, then got back on my way.

The next town was Morley, which was a vestige of small-town Americana, the kind of place where people decorated their yards with old tractors and American flags.

The walking continued to be good. The roads were smooth, with wide, flat shoulders. The air smelled sweet and was alive with the cacophonous song of insects. One peculiar thing I noticed was that along one long stretch all the power poles were bent toward the road at a fifteen-degree angle.

By late afternoon I reached Sikeston, which I quickly deduced was a religious community as I passed nine churches on the way into town. I ate dinner at Jay's Krispy Fried Chicken, then, following my waitress's advice, walked to the other side of town and booked a room at the Days Inn.

CHAPTER

Twenty-two

Our culture's quest to hide death behind
a facade of denial has made fools and
pretended immortals of us all. Perhaps it
would be more helpful and liberating to
begin each day by repeating the words of
Crazy Horse, "Today is a good day to die."

Alan Christoffersen's diary

The next day began pleasantly enough, with ideal weather and open cotton fields, the air fragrant with the smell of cotton.

I stopped and picked a boll, just to see what picking cotton was like. Fiddling with it as I walked, it took me nearly fifteen minutes to liberate the seeds from the plant, which did more to explain to me the historical impact of the cotton gin than a whole middle school semester studying the Civil War.

Around noon I suddenly got a strange, sick feeling that something was wrong. I stopped and looked around. I was alone, miles from the nearest town. I took off my hat and wiped the sweat from my forehead. Had I forgotten something? Was it a premonition? I hadn't felt anything like that since . . . It came to me. It was one year ago from that very hour that McKale had broken her back. I put my hat back on and kept on walking.

·✦·

After eighteen miles I reached the town of New Madrid (pronounced MAD-rid), which seemed more southern to me than northern.

Of all the Civil War states, Missouri was, perhaps, the

most complicated. Politically bipolar. Officially, the state was pro-Union, but many, if not most, of its residents were Confederate or sympathetic to the South's cause.

A mile into town I turned off onto Dawson Road, where I ate dinner at the local eatery, Taster's Restaurant, then, at my waitress's recommendation, walked to the Hunter-Dawson State Historic Site.

The Hunter-Dawson house is a monument to the life-style enjoyed by wealthy southern families in the late 1800s. The fifteen-room mansion was built by William and Amanda Hunter, owners of a successful mercantile business that capitalized on New Madrid's location on the Mississippi River. William died of yellow fever before the home was completed, but Amanda and her seven children moved into the house in 1860, and the home remained in the family for more than a century until it was purchased by the city of New Madrid and restored to the 1860–80 period. Today it contains the Hunters' original furniture as well as family portraits and a large portion of the family's library.

I walked to the site's visitor center, a long trailer planted directly across the street from the mansion. The guide, a young female park worker wearing a baseball cap, informed me that it was nearly closing time but that she'd give me an abbreviated tour of the mansion free of charge.

The Hunter family had owned thirty-six slaves. During the Civil War, New Madrid leaned heavily toward the Confederate cause, and one of the Hunter sons joined the Confederate Army. During the Siege of New Madrid by Union forces, the mansion was occupied by General Pope and one of the Hunter boys joined the Union Army to keep the family home from being burned.

In one of the upstairs rooms there was a display of

mourning dresses, bonnets and armbands. I was told that at the loss of a family member, women wore the black dresses for two years, while men wore black armbands for three to six months. My guide explained that mourning was much more formalized back then and that even Queen Victoria had mourned the loss of her husband, Prince Albert, for forty years. It made me wonder why modern culture has so painstakingly removed the rituals of death. Today, society pressures the bereaved to sweep their grief under the carpet of normality—the sooner the better.

When the tour concluded, I tipped my guide, then walked back to the street while she locked her office, then drove away. After she was gone, I returned to the home and pitched my tent on the soft grass beneath the maple, oak, and walnut trees behind the house.

CHAPTER

Twenty-three

You can tell as much about a
culture from their diet as from their
literature. Sometimes, perhaps, more.

Alan Christoffersen's diary

My headache and exhaustion returned the next day, and I didn't walk far, barely sixteen miles, stopping at a hotel called Pattie's Inn. The first thing I noticed was the large NO PETS ALLOWED warning on the hotel's marquee. Then, just in case you missed it, there was another NO PETS sign on the hotel's front door. I walked into the hotel's lobby and there was yet another NO PETS sign on the wall behind the check-in counter, with, oddly, a dog lying on the floor beneath it.

The next morning I felt better again. As I walked back to the highway, I came upon a young man standing near the freeway on-ramp with a large handwritten poster-board sign around his neck. As I got closer, I read the board.

I CHEATED ON MY WIFE.
THIS IS MY PUNISHMENT.

I stopped a couple yards from him, read his sign, then looked up at him. He was red-faced with embarrassment and just stood there, avoiding eye contact. After a moment I said, "She made you do that?"

Glancing furtively at me, he said, "Yeah."

"For how long?"

"Today. And all day tomorrow."

I shook my head, then continued walking.

Highway 61 South turned into a bigger, busier road with a speed limit of seventy miles per hour. Fortunately it had a wide shoulder. I kept thinking back on the guy with the sign around his neck and chuckling.

I crossed into Pemiscot County and left the highway for a frontage road lined with cotton fields. Four hours into my walk I stopped at Chubby's BBQ for lunch.

South of the Mason-Dixon line, barbecue restaurants are as plentiful as deviled eggs at a church picnic. In the same vein that the state of Washington prides itself on the creative naming of coffee shops, the South holds the titling of barbecue joints in high regard. I dedicated a page in my journal to writing down some of their names.

Fat Matt's

Kiss My Ribs

Squat and Gobble

Swett's

Bubba's

Porkpies

Birds, Butts and Bones

The Boneyard

The Bonelicker

—

Barbecutie

Butts

Bubbalous Bodacious Barbeque

Dixie Pig

Bone Daddy

Prissy Polly's

Pig Pickins Parlor

The Boars' Butts

The Prancing Pig

Holy Smokes (A bbq joint in a converted
Lutheran church)

Sticky Lips

Adam's Rib

The Rib Cage

The Butt Rub

The Pig Out Inn

Hog Wild

Half Porked

Lord of the Swine

Big D's Piggy Strut

The Swinery

Some of the restaurants' slogans were noteworthy as well.

"We shall sell no swine before its time."

"A waist is a terrible thing to mind."

"No pig left behind."

After a lunch of chopped brisket, collard greens and cheesy mashed potatoes, I returned to the interstate. I disliked walking such a busy road. The draft created by semis traveling at seventy-plus miles per hour would hit my pack like wind against a schooner's sail and almost knock me over. Twice I lost my Akubra hat, chasing it across more than one lane of traffic. Still, I made decent time and after twenty-six miles I took exit 8 off 61 and walked to the Deerfield Inn. For dinner I ate a meatball sandwich and a tuna salad at the local Subway restaurant.

CHAPTER

Twenty-four

Missouri calls itself the "Show
Me" state. I'm not sure if they're
claiming skepticism or voyeurism.

Alan Christoffersen's diary

The next morning I reached the town of Steele in less than an hour. Running parallel to the road was a slow-moving train, and I saw several men clambering onto the outside of one of the cars. The scene reminded me of Israel, the hitchhiker I had met outside Marceline, Missouri, which now seemed like a decade ago. It was hard to believe that after all these months I was still in the same state. But not for much longer. Just before noon I saw a small arch spanning the road in front of me. As I approached, I could see that it had the word ARKANSAS written across it.

A hundred yards from the border, I passed a dilapidated white house with a plaque in front of it. I stopped to read it.

EDGAR HAROLD LLOYD
MEDAL OF HONOR RECIPIENT FROM WWII

It was a poor monument, but a monument just the same, and the fact that a hero came from such an unassuming locale made me glad.

Like my transcendent experience of crossing from Wyoming to South Dakota, shortly after crossing the Arkansas state line, the landscape and architecture improved and soon I was walking past country club estates with beautiful manicured lawns and minicolonial mansions. I stopped for lunch in the town of Blytheville, where I ate southern fried chicken.

Unfortunately, not far past the restaurant, the scenery changed from beautiful mini-mansions to pawnshops and boarded-up buildings, making me think the place was only Blytheville for some. I walked another five miles and spent the night at the Best Western Blytheville Inn. That evening I turned on my cell phone to check for messages. No one had called.

CHAPTER

Twenty-five

To challenge the rules of conventionality
is to open ourselves to an entirely
new universe. One cannot pioneer
new worlds from old trails.

Alan Christoffersen's diary

The next day felt like a rerun of earlier days, with seemingly endless cotton fields and, again, the mysteriously leaning power lines. The tilt of the poles was so perfectly symmetrical that I wondered if they had been purposely set in this manner or if their leaning was caused by some natural phenomenon, like the famed bell tower of Pisa. I vowed to ask someone when I got the chance, which settled my mind on the matter enough that I never actually got around to asking anyone.

I felt physically more able than I had in days and I was eager to get through this lonely stretch, so I walked nearly twenty-five miles until I reached the quaint little town of Wilson. Wilson had once been a thriving logging town, built around a huge sawmill and lumber yard which, decades before, had been closed down, cordoned off by an eight-foot chain-link fence topped with razor wire.

What distinguished Wilson from the other towns along that stretch was the architecture—which, peculiarly, was more British than southern. I stopped for dinner at the Wilson Café and my server gave me some of the history. The town was founded by Robert E. Lee Wilson, who, after cutting down the trees, used the land for agricultural purposes. Wilson pretty much owned the town, but he was a generous public benefactor, and every town resident had use of the company doctor for just $1.25 annually, about $17 in today's money.

Wilson's son, Wilson Jr., and his bride, returned from a honeymoon to England fascinated by British architecture. Apparently their excitement was contagious, because shortly thereafter all the town's buildings were either built or retrofitted with Tudor elements, giving the town a distinct and charming British appearance.

I finished my meal of split-pea soup and pork ribs, then camped the night behind a screen of trees in the park next to the restaurant.

CHAPTER

Twenty-six

For centuries the spiritually seeking have
asked God for a sign. Perhaps that's
why there's so many of them planted
out front of southern churches.

Alan Christoffersen's diary

The next day marked two weeks since I'd resumed my walk. Unremarkably, I passed more cotton fields and walked through a string of small towns: Bassett, Joiner and Frenchmans Bayou (the latter town so named because no one could pronounce the French name the original French settler had given it).

My route led to Highway 77, which I reached just before sunset. I ate fried chicken and Baskin-Robbins ice cream I bought at a gas station, then stopped for the night at the small town of Clarkedale, making camp on the far side of the railroad tracks that ran parallel to the highway. I set my tent too close to the tracks, and when a train whistled in the middle of the night, I woke, all but certain my life was over. I slept fitfully the rest of the night, anticipating the advent of another passing train, which never came.

Early the next morning I reached a town with the biblically inspired name of Jericho. Appropriately, the first street I passed was Praise the Lord Boulevard. Perhaps not so appropriately, the first building I passed was the Jericho Liquor Store. I was always surprised to see more than one church in a town with so few residents, and this town contained many. I walked by a church sign that seemed especially apropos to my circumstance:

Are you on the right road?

I should write something about church signs. Walking from Seattle—the third-*least* Christian city in America—to the pious southern roads of the Bible Belt, one of the things that stood out to me (in addition to the sheer number of churches) was the phenomenon of church signs. Pretty much all of the churches had signs or marquees. Some were designed to lure people to their meetings, while others were sermons unto themselves. A few of them bordered on the bizarre.

As I had with the Wall Drug signs along Interstate 90 in South Dakota, I decided to dedicate a few pages of my diary to writing down some of these messages.

Walmart is not the only saving place.

God's last name isn't "damn"!

Stop, drop and roll won't work in Hell.

You have one New Friend Request.
From Jesus. Confirm or Ignore.

Santa Claus never died for anyone.

Don't make me come down there.—God.

Read the Bible.
It will scare the Hell out of you.

Yes, our A/C is out.
But there's no A/C in hell either!

Free Coffee. Everlasting life.
Membership has its privileges.

Life is a puzzle.
Look here for the missing PEACE.

Forbidden fruits create many jams.

God is like TIDE soap.
He gets the stains out others left behind.

Why pay for GPS?
Jesus gives direction for free.

Honk if you love Jesus.
Text while driving if you want to meet Him.

What is missing from CH**CH? U R

There are some questions
that can't be answered by Google.

Be an organ donor.
Give your heart to Jesus.

Sign broke. Message inside.

A Step of Faith

People use duct tape to fix everything.
God uses nails.

Prayer isn't the only thing
that can bring you to your knees.

For all you do, His blood's for you.

Then there were some that could only be described as bizarre.

Don't let worries kill you.
Let the church help.

Jesus said, "Bring me that ass."

To ERR is human. To ARRRRR is Pirate.

Face powder may get a man, but
it takes baking powder to keep him.

God does not believe in Atheists.
Therefore Atheists do not exist.

Midnight Mass and Toga Party. B.Y.O.B.J.
(Bring your own Baby Jesus)

7 pm Hymn singing. Come prepared to sin.

Keep using my name in vain.
I'll make rush hour longer.—God

Before noon I passed through Marion, a town with a sizable population, then changed roads to Interstate 55 leading to Memphis.

The road into Memphis wouldn't have been easy even if I had been at my physical peak. I had a long and difficult day walking, more than twenty-six city miles. Despite my exhaustion, I kept on because I didn't feel safe enough to camp anywhere. The outskirts of Memphis are a blighted landscape of gutted buildings and stockyards.

When I finally reached the city, I booked a room at the first hotel I came to, the Super 7 Inn Graceland on Brooks Road. I could tell that it was a rough area from the inch-thick, bulletproof partition between me and the angry-looking Indian man working at the reception counter.

Once I was in my room, I found Paige's phone number and called, but my cell went straight to voicemail. I wondered if her grandmother had died. I left my phone number for when she was ready to talk. I wondered if I would ever hear from her again.

I was too exhausted to leave my room, so I ate an entire box of Pop-Tarts and fell asleep.

CHAPTER

Twenty-seven

Elvis may have left the building, but some
of the audience have kept their seats.

Alan Christoffersen's diary

The next morning both my head and body ached, which I attributed to pushing myself too hard the day before. Still, I got up earlier than usual, as I planned to put in a normal day of walking but also wanted to take the time to see Graceland, Elvis Presley's mansion, which had been turned into a museum.

I took a quick shower, dressed, then fled the dumpy little hotel.

It wasn't hard to find Graceland. In Memphis, all roads lead to Elvis. At the first block I made a right on Elvis Presley Boulevard, then, following the abundant signage, walked a little more than a mile to Elvis's mecca.

I have a confession to make, one that I fully realize may lessen me in your eyes. *I don't really like Elvis's music.* Before you abandon me on the side of Elvis Presley Boulevard, let me clarify my position. I'm not saying that I don't like *Elvis*. I do. Actually, I like the *idea* of Elvis. And I think that if more people were completely honest, they'd admit the same thing. Elvis is much more than his music, he's the image, the flash, the iridescent sparkle of rhinestones, the entire American dream wrapped up in a lip-curling, pelvis-gyrating, hunk-a-burnin'-love. Elvis succeeded because we *wanted* him to succeed—a God-fearing young man from a sharecroppers' shack speaking out for a generation of American youth with an ingratiating "yes, sir," and "yes, ma'am." Of course the fact that women, young and old, found him insanely good-looking didn't hurt any.

Only in walking through Memphis can one truly realize the extent of the adulation bestowed on the young man from Tupelo who sold a billion records and inspired ten thousand impersonators. Elvis was more than an entertainer—he was divinity in rhinestones. It would not surprise me in the least if someday, perhaps a century from now, a religion springs forth from his legacy. The Church of Elvis. Its followers would wear pompadours, dress in holy white leather rhinestone-studded robes, and resolve to "love each other tender." The theological possibilities are endless. Hell would be referred to as the Heartbreak Hotel, and at funerals the Elvisian minister would say, "Brother Jones has left the building," "He's joined the choir," or "He's off to the Graceland in the sky."

Graceland wasn't open yet, so I ate breakfast at the adjacent Rock & Roll Café, then waited outside the park in a growing line of Elvis fans. When I got inside the visitor center, I bought a ticket for the whole tour, which included Graceland, Elvis's auto museum, and his two airplanes.

Graceland is marvelously kitsch, preserved in full seventies splendor, with a black baby grand piano on white carpet, red fur, leopard skin, a jungle room with an indoor waterfall, and stained-glass peacocks. Words like "gaudy," "garish," "tacky" and "tasteless" come to mind.

McKale would have laughed herself silly. She would have said something like, "It looks like a Liberace nightmare." I just thought it was cool. The experience was worth the admission. Heck, it was worth the walk to Memphis.

After the Graceland tour, I took the shuttle over to the

auto museum and planes. The Elvis Presley Car Museum houses more than thirty of Elvis's vehicles, including his famous pink Cadillac, Stutz Blackhawks, a 1975 Dino Ferrari, two Rolls-Royce (one black, one white), a six-door Mercedes limousine, Harley-Davidson motorcycles and the John Deere tractor Elvis drove at Graceland.

Elvis also had two airplanes. His largest, the *Lisa Marie* (named after his daughter), was a 1958 Corvair 880. Elvis spent nearly a million dollars remodeling the plane with a living room, conference room, sitting room and a private bedroom.

Not to be outdone by Graceland's kitsch, the airplane has leather-topped tables and suede chairs, a television and telephone, gold-specked bathroom sinks and 24-karat gold-plated safety belts.

His second plane was a smaller Lockheed JetStar, less impressive, but also customized by Elvis with a yellow and green interior.

Finally, succumbing to the commercial allure of the shrine, I broke down and purchased a Graceland T-shirt, then set off, walking south down the bustling boulevard back to Highway 51 South. An hour later I crossed the state border into Mississippi.

CHAPTER

Twenty-eight

Some towns, like people, seem to
attract history. I suppose this is as
much a curse as it is a blessing.

Alan Christoffersen's diary

Over the next six days I followed Highway 51 south to Batesville, then walked east on Highway 278. Tolkien wrote that easy times do not make good stories, which is why I have little to write about that part of my journey. The pleasant exception was my stop in Oxford, a historic town between Batesville and Tupelo.

Oxford is a picturesque college town, home of the University of Mississippi (aka "Ole Miss") and laden with history.

During the Civil War, Oxford was invaded by Generals Sherman, Grant, and Andrew Jackson Smith, the latter of which left his mark by burning the buildings in the town square. Oxford is also the hometown of American writer and Nobel Prize Laureate William Faulkner, who based several of his novels on the small town.

In 1962, Oxford gained national attention twice, first when Faulkner died, then, later that fall, when Mississippi state officials attempted to prevent James Meredith, a black man, from entering the university.

U.S. Attorney General Robert F. Kennedy ordered federal marshals to escort Meredith to school. In response, thousands of protestors rioted, damaging property and killing two men, one of whom was a French journalist sent to cover the affair.

President Kennedy responded by mobilizing the National Guard, which restored order to the small town. Meredith enrolled without further incident and eventually completed his degree, though he was constantly harassed and spent the rest of his time at the university with U.S. marshal bodyguards who escorted him from class to class.

Today, Oxford is a vibrant, charming town patterned after its British namesake, with a bustling town square complete with London-inspired double-decker tourist buses and red telephone booths.

Encouraged by the temperate weather, I spent a leisurely day in the town. I rode the double-decker bus, ate lunch in the town square at the Ajax Diner, browsed books at the famous Square Books bookstore, then spent the rest of the afternoon at Rowan Oak, Faulkner's home turned museum. I thought it might be interesting to camp somewhere on the twenty-nine-acre estate, but discovered that the site was as well guarded as it was maintained. I spent the night closer to the highway.

✵

I suppose it was destiny that my road south led through Elvis's hometown of Tupelo, a route I traveled in reverse of the path the King took to global stardom. Five days from Memphis I exited the Appalachian Highway into Tupelo.

Tupelo is a sleepy, brittle town, little more than a memorial to Elvis's life. Not surprisingly, its downtown was decorated with vinyl banners silk-screened with heroic-sized images of Elvis's face.

Less heralded than the King's birthplace is the site of

the Civil War Battle of Tupelo, a standoff between Union General Andrew Jackson Smith and confederate General Nathan Bedford Forrest. At that point in the conflict, the tide had already turned on the South and it was the last time Forrest's troops would see war.

It was dark when I reached the city center, so I ate dinner at Romie's Barbeque and booked a room at the Hilton Garden Inn.

CHAPTER

Twenty-nine

Today I walked through Tupelo, Elvis's
birthplace. Those who wish a magnified
life should remember that no one is born
great. No one. Every entertainer began
in the audience. This is encouraging.
Elvis began life in a sharecropper's shack.
Lincoln, a log cabin. Jesus a manger.

Alan Christoffersen's diary

The next morning I ate the hotel's complimentary breakfast, which, in addition to the standard fare, also included
grits. After breakfast I walked to Elvis's birthplace.

Elvis's home was tiny, a sharecropper's shack, about a
tenth the size of the museum built to celebrate it. In its
day the home cost $180 to construct and was built with
borrowed money. The Presley family lived there until
Elvis's father, Vernon, was sent to jail for eight months for
forging a check (he had altered the amount from $4 to
$14) and the home was lost. Elvis repurchased the home
and property the same year he bought Graceland.

I didn't spend much time in Tupelo, just long enough
to get the rest of Elvis's story, then, avoiding the interstate, headed south on Highway 6 toward 278, then east,
crossing into Alabama. My route led me through two
of the most peculiarly named towns I had encountered,
the neighboring municipalities of Guin and Gu-win. I
sensed there was a story there, so I asked an employee
of a Guin gas mart how the towns got their names. I was
told that the town of Guin, with a population of less than
a thousand, was seeking to annex the neighboring town
of Ear Gap. (Really, who comes up with these names?)
The owner of the drive-in theater in Ear Gap—a justifi-

ably influential man in a town of less than a hundred—was about to put up a new sign at his theater, so he lobbied to change the town name to Gu-win, close enough to Guin that he wouldn't have to change his sign if the annexation went through. The town's name change succeeded, but the annexation failed.

Highway 278 intersected with Interstate 78, a busier, but better-constructed road, which took me southeast into the heart of Birmingham. I walked through Homewood (the site of Red Mountain with its famous Vulcan statue—the largest cast-iron statue in the world) and Vestavia Hills, stopping for the day in Hoover.

Birmingham is Alabama's largest city and, like all metropolitan areas, wasn't the easiest walking. Still, Birmingham has a welcoming southern ambience that made me glad to be there. I considered staying an extra day, but eventually decided to keep on walking.

If someone had told me what I would encounter on the next leg of my journey, I never would have believed them.

C H A P T E R

Thirty

Those willing to trade freedom for
certainty are certain to find the
cure worse than the ailment.

Alan Christoffersen's diary

My next target destination, Montgomery, Alabama, was a little more than ninety miles south of Birmingham, which, health willing, I could make in four days at a reasonable pace. Departing Birmingham from Hoover, I walked twenty miles the first day to the little town of Pasqua, then, feeling strong, followed up with a grueling twenty-four miles to Clanton and almost sixteen miles the third day to a tiny dot on my map called Pine Flat. Actually, I didn't quite make it to Pine Flat. As my day wound down, about a mile before I reached my day's walking goal, I had one of the strangest and most frightening experiences of my entire walk—one that haunts me to this day.

In the flammeous, retreating light of a fading day, it took me a moment to be sure of what I was looking at. Or maybe it was just my difficulty in believing it. There, in the middle of nowhere, about twenty yards back from the road near a grove of dogwoods, a woman was tied by her wrists to a tree. She was young and reasonably attractive, in her mid-twenties, with long, golden hair that rested on her shoulders. She was partially obscured by the tree, and had it not been for the bright yellow T-shirt she wore, I might not have seen her at all.

I couldn't make sense of the situation. The woman

wasn't struggling nor did she seem distressed. I briefly looked around to make sure there wasn't anyone else nearby before I crept toward her.

When I was ten yards away, I asked, "Are you okay?"

I startled her. She looked at me warily. Silently.

After a moment I said, "You're tied up."

She didn't respond.

"Do you need help?"

Still nothing.

I looked around me, then walked closer, wondering if she were perhaps deaf. "Would you like me to untie you?" I said, making gestures to my own wrists.

"Stay away," she barked.

I hadn't expected that response. "Why are you tied to a tree?"

"My master tied me here."

"Your master?"

"Master El."

I *definitely* hadn't expected that response. "Is Master El going to untie you too?"

"If it is His will."

"I don't understand."

"That's because you are of this world."

I stood there wondering what to do when someone said, "It wouldn't matter if I cut her loose, she still wouldn't leave."

At the sound of the voice the woman gasped. I turned to see a tall, thick-lipped, redheaded man walking toward us. ". . . Would you, dear?"

The woman bowed as far as her constraints allowed. "Please forgive me, Master. This Earthman spoke to me."

"You're forgiven, KaEl." He turned to me. "KaEl *asked* to be tied to the tree. Isn't that true, KaEl?"

"Yes, Master."

"Why would she do that?" I asked.

"She feared that in a moment of weakness her carnal self would rebel and she might run away, so she wisely asked for help. But I don't think she really needs it. She's been very obedient."

"Thank you, Master."

He turned to face her. "How goes your purification?"

"The flesh is weak, Master. But the spirit is willing."

I looked back and forth between the two of them. Part of me wanted to bolt, the other part wasn't willing to abandon the young woman. "Why is she tied to the tree?" I asked.

"I just told you," the man said curtly.

I rephrased my question. "Why is she standing here?"

"She's learning to overcome the carnal nature within. She's on the last twelve hours of her five-day purification and submission."

"Submission?"

"Each member of our society must purge the world from their heart by undergoing the purification and submission ritual. It's a privilege. She forgoes earthly food for five days and drinks only blessed, holy water mixed with frankincense. During this time she cannot speak to anyone but her Master. Unfortunately, you interfered with her sanctification."

"I didn't know."

"Don't worry, I can absolve her of her commission. Our religion is not without mercy."

"Religion? This is a church?"

"Not *a* church. *The* church. We are the church of the AhnEl."

I looked at him quizzically. "I've never heard of it."

"You have now."

"What kind of church are you?"

A slight smile lifted the corners of his mouth. "We are a pearl of great price—a rarity of rarities. A church of truth."

"What kind of truths?"

"The word is not plural. There is one truth, simple and unified, and millions of extrapolations, subterfuges and delusions."

"Tell me about this . . . *truth*."

He crossed his arms, his gaze leveling on me. "Are you prepared to receive it? I have neither the time nor inclination to cast pearls before swine."

His arrogance surprised me. "Try me," I said.

"If you have ears to hear, you may ask me anything."

"Does your church believe in the Bible?"

"Do we believe *in* the Bible, or do we believe *the* Bible? Be specific."

"Do you believe the Bible to be the word of God?"

He grinned. "Now that's a question. The answer closest to your intent is yes. Of course we do. Not that it's *His* word. It's not. *He* didn't write it. But we do know that it's a record of His teachings and history. But, unlike the rest of the Bible-blind world, we actually *understand* the book."

Again, I was taken aback by his arrogance. "You don't believe that anyone, besides you, understands the Bible."

"I'm quite certain of it," he said. "For centuries, before Gutenberg came along, the clergy hid the Bible from the people. Today, the people shroud it in mystery and hide it from themselves.

"You see, the Bible must be understood in context. The Bible is true, at least it was in its earliest, unadulterated renditions. It's common knowledge, or should be, that through time there have been tens of thousands of alterations to the Bible. In fact, there have been more words changed in the book than there are words. But, that aside, even assuming that it was all truth and preserved as such, it would still only be true within the realm of its authors' experiences, since all writing is tainted by the context of the writer."

"What do you mean?"

"Allow me to explain it this way. If an aborigine should find a radio and hear a voice coming from it, he might say that there is a spirit in the strange box. He isn't being deceitful, he's just explaining his experience from what he understands. Even if he were to break the radio open and examine its parts, he still couldn't possibly understand what he sees—the circuit boards and transistors that make the sound possible. His explanation doesn't make him a liar, it's the best he can do given his cultural and educational limitations. The interpreters of the Bible are the same as this poor aborigine."

After a moment I said, "That makes sense."

The man smiled, pleased with my answer. "KaEl, could it be that we have found an Earthman who is more interested in truth than patching up the holes in his own leaking belief system?" He took a few steps toward me. "What is your name?"

"Alan."

"I am Master El. You may call me El. Why are you wandering the world, Alan?"

I didn't want to tell him. "I'm just walking."

He examined my pack. "Where are you walking to?"

"Key West, Florida."

"Where did you begin your journey?"

"Seattle."

"You've walked the whole distance?"

I nodded.

"Then you are a man with stories. I would like to hear them. A man who has walked all day must be hungry. Come dine with me."

For a moment I said nothing, hesitant to go anywhere with a religious nut who would tie someone to a tree. "I have food," I said.

"I'm sure you do, but, if you're eating from your pack, I guarantee I can do better. I'll make you a deal. I'll provide you with a hot meal and you can tell me of your travels. Agreed?" He put out his hand.

I just looked at him.

"Come on, Alan. You have nothing to fear. I may be sly as a serpent but I'm harmless as a dove. Come with me and I will feed you—body and, should you desire, soul."

"Where do you live?" I asked.

"Just a mile or so from here," he said pointing east. "I have a vehicle."

I thought a moment more, then my curiosity got the better of me. "All right."

"Splendid," he said. "Splendid." He turned toward the woman. "We will leave you to your quest. The celestial spirit abide with you, KaEl."

She bowed her head. "Praise be to my Master."

.⋇.

I followed him about twenty yards to his car, a brand-new Range Rover with the paper dealer plate still in the window. Kyle Craig had owned a similar model. I knew enough about the vehicle to know it was worth more than a hundred thousand dollars.

"You can lay your pack on the back seat," he said.

I started feeling hesitant again, wondering what I

had gotten myself into, but still I opened the back door and set my pack inside. I climbed into the passenger's seat.

El started his car and pulled out of the grove onto a dirt road, which we followed back for nearly two miles.

"How far have you walked today?" El asked.

"About sixteen miles."

"Is that how far you walk every day?"

"I usually try for twenty. Sometimes more."

"You must be in very good physical condition."

"Walking twenty-five hundred miles will do that," I said.

"Indeed it would."

We drove almost ten minutes before we came to a fenced compound consisting of a large, rustic-looking red barn, an A-framed house and two log buildings. A garden and a vineyard ran the length of the front fence.

There was a guard booth near the compound's front entrance and the gate opened at our approach. El pulled the car to the front of the barn and put it in park, leaving the vehicle idling. A muscular young man wearing the same style of yellow T-shirt as the woman at the tree ran out of the building as if he'd been waiting for El's return.

"This is where we'll be dining," El said.

The man stood at attention as El handed him the car keys. "Welcome home, Master," the man said.

"Thank you, MarkEl," he replied.

El walked around the side of the car where I was standing. "Follow me," he said.

I opened the back door to retrieve my backpack.

"You can leave it," El said. "It will be safe."

I pulled it out anyway. "I would be more comfortable having it with me."

He looked annoyed, but said, "Whatever makes you more comfortable."

I shut the car door and the man pulled the vehicle away, disappearing around the side of the barn. Behind us the large gates shut. I wondered if I was a prisoner. I thought about the gun my father had given me, stowed in the bottom of my pack.

"This way," El said, motioning to an open door.

I followed him inside. Even though the building looked rustic on the outside, inside it was clean and nicely furnished in a modern European style. The high-ceilinged room was spacious and open and three of its walls were painted with murals. The largest wall depicted the moai statues of Easter Island, while the other two were of the Egyptian Pyramids and the Mayan Pyramids of Tikal. The vaulted ceiling was painted dark blue, with constellations, and the exaggerated stars had eyeballs in their centers. The floor was hardwood, with areas covered by rugs.

Most surprising to me was that the room was filled with people, maybe forty or more, all dressed in the same yellow T-shirts. They all stared at us as we entered, looking curiously at me. I felt like a stray their "master" had brought home. Near the center of the room were two long dining tables. As we entered, El said to a young man with long, dark blue hair, "DarEl, bring us something to eat."

"Yes, Master. What would please my Master?"

"Surprise us," he said. The young man quickly disappeared behind a white door splattered with blue and red paint. "Come," El said to me, gesturing. Every eye in the room was still on us as I followed him to the first table.

"Sit. Please," he said.

We sat down on a long bench lined with red vinyl cushions.

A stunningly beautiful redheaded woman walked up to us and knelt in front of El. "How may I serve my Master?"

"Bring us something to drink," El replied. "My usual. And some tea. What will you have?" he asked me.

"Just water," I said.

She glanced at me, then back at El. "Yes, Master." She leaned down and kissed his feet, then stood, hurrying off behind the white door. I watched in amazement. El seemed used to such adoration.

The man with blue hair quickly returned, carrying a bowl of red hummus and a stoneware plate piled with pita bread.

"Your service is accepted, DarEl."

The man smiled. "Thank you, Master. Praise Master."

El motioned to the bowl. "Eat. It's quite good. It's hummus with red chili." He dipped a triangular piece of bread into the bowl, scooping up a dollop of hummus. "Tell me, Alan, before you were a sojourner, what did you do?"

Just then the redheaded woman returned carrying our drinks on a tray. She set a glass of red wine on the table in front of El, followed by a teacup and a teapot. She poured the tea, then put in a spoonful of sugar, stirred it, then looked at El. "May I serve my master anything else?"

"I am satisfied, my dear. Your service is accepted."

"Thank you," she said. She handed me a glass of water, knelt again and kissed El's feet, then took the tray and walked away. I waited until El looked back at me.

"I was in advertising," I said.

He nodded. "We are in similar fields then. We both are engineers of the mind. Are you a religious man?"

"Not particularly."

"Do you believe in a God?"

"Yes."

"Do *you* believe in the Bible?"

"Yes. I think so."

"You *think* so?" He gazed intently into my eyes. "Have you even read it?"

"Parts," I admitted.

He shook his head condescendingly. *"Parts,"* he said. "Then you do not really believe it. Or, at least, that it might lead to your eternal salvation. Otherwise you would cling to it as an overboard sailor clings to a life ring." He lifted his glass of wine and drank. "Unlike you, I've read the Bible more times than I can remember. I'm more fascinated by it each time I read it. As I said before, the truth of the Bible must be understood in context."

He leaned toward me. "The Bible is as ancient as time, but more modern than ours. To the enlightened, the book describes spaceships and interstellar beings, rocket launches, weapons of mass destruction, holograms and, most importantly, the origin of the species."

"What species?" I asked.

"Our species, of course. You see, the Garden of Eden, Adam and Eve, it's all truth, contextually shaded, but as truthful as today's newspaper." He grinned. "Actually, given the state of today's media bias, more truthful. In fact, DNA evidence has proven conclusively that our entire species descended from a single female. This isn't conjecture, it's proven fact. The idea that mankind gradually descended from monkeys is intellectually absurd. What do you think of that?"

"I think most scientists would disagree with you."

He smiled. "Only the foolish ones. You see, scientists are just as dogmatic as the religious. Maybe more so. They rarely change their minds, they just die off and the next generation's thinking emerges. The difference between them and me is that I have a viable explanation for the species and they don't.

"You see, even the most ardent Darwinist must admit that there is a fundamental flaw in his belief when it comes to the evolution of human beings. For millions of years, hominids, a half-ape, half-man beast, roamed the world. Then suddenly, boom"—he flourished his hands dramatically—"there are homo sapiens. Intelligent, self-aware, language-speaking beings capable of building pyramids, advancing complex mathematical formulas, understanding advanced aerodynamics and mapping the universe. They even performed successful brain surgery. Yes, there was successful brain surgery more than a thousand years ago. We have the archeological evidence."

He shook his head. "What a culture we live in. We are swimming in an ocean of information, and drowning in ignorance. In the late 1800s archeologists discovered the ancient Sumerian cuneiform texts, writings of earth's oldest-known civilization. When scholars translated their writings, what they discovered surprised them. The Sumerian tablets actually agreed with the Old Testament; the genesis of the earth, the Garden of Eden, even the story of Noah and the Great Flood. Of course, even the oldest Chinese writings, carved into tortoiseshells, tell of the great flood. You do believe in Noah and his ark, don't you?"

"Not literally," I said.

His brow fell with disappointment. "If not literally, then how?"

"Noah's ark isn't feasible. You couldn't carry that many creatures and their food in a boat ten times the size the Bible describes."

El grinned. "You could, of course, if you were carrying their DNA."

"DNA?"

"Exactly. Truth, my friend, is found in the gray space between religion and science."

"DNA wasn't discovered until the 1950s."

"No, that's when it was *re*discovered. We modern humans want to believe that we are at the pinnacle of evolution and intellectual thought." He said this with a mocking grin. "So we conveniently ignore everything counter to that belief, including architectural marvels that are thousands of years old that we cannot duplicate today. We are not more intelligent. Greater cultures have lived and died, not just in the universe, but on this planet.

"Did you know that in 1913 a farmer in a tiny South African town called Boskop discovered a skull unlike anything anyone had seen before? It was so unusual that it made its way to the top scientists and anthropologists around the world. What was so unusual about the skull was its dimensions. The skull was larger than ours, but its face was smaller. In fact, it was less apelike than we are. You might have seen these pictures—they're the same face we see in people's descriptions of today's aliens.

"At first, scientists thought that these skulls might be an anomaly, an aberration, caused by a disease, like hydrocephalus, or some such thing. But this theory was quickly disproven when scores of similar skulls were discovered.

"These beings had brains twenty-five percent larger than ours. Scientists estimate that their average IQ would be close to 150, which means, on average, they were geniuses." He leaned forward. "Do you understand what I'm saying? They were smarter than us. They were more

advanced than us. We are an intellectual step backward."
He leaned forward again. "If you still haven't caught my
deeper meaning, let me spell it out for you, Alan. *They*
were not us. We are not alone." He studied my eyes for
my reaction. "The evidence is everywhere, carved into
the records of our earth. On every continent there are
carvings and hieroglyphs of spacemen and spaceships.
They are described in great detail in the Bible. Just open
to Ezekiel."

"You're talking about aliens," I said. "You believe in
UFOs?"

"My belief system isn't predicated on faith. I have *knowl-edge*. And the term UFO is a misnomer. The crafts you're
referring to aren't really *unidentified* flying objects if they've
been identified, are they?"

"Are you saying that you've seen them?" I asked.

"Seen them, touched them, with gloves, of course,
they're remarkably hot once they've traveled in our atmo-sphere, I've even been inside them. But it's not the crafts—
it's the pilots I find most intriguing. Seeing them for the
first time, if you don't wet yourself, is a mind flush. Trust
me, everything you think you know about the world is
immediately down the toilet. The first time I saw them, it
took me days to stop shaking."

I just looked at him.

"Of course you're skeptical. It's safer that way. But be-lieve me, they are as real as you or me."

"You're telling me that you've seen an alien from an-other planet?"

He smiled. "I've sat in councils with them. I would say
that we are, intellectually, like children next to them, but
I would be doing them a disservice in the representation.
We are more like apes, our spiritual and mental develop-

ment so rudimentary, it would be like enrolling a chimpanzee in advanced Harvard physics and theology classes. Their translators speak our crude language so exquisitely, it's like listening to Mozart." He leaned forward. "Let me teach you something, Alan. Have you ever wondered why it is that whenever there's a major technical breakthrough, it seems to appear around the globe at the same time— advancements like the pyramids, the airplane, the electric filament or radio waves? That's because when the Guardians believe our species is ready to advance the idea is released to us."

"Guardians?"

"That's what I call them, but that's only because our inefficient language doesn't have the proper title for them. They call themselves the Ahn, which roughly means 'parent' or 'enlightened caregiver.' But most people just call them God. The truth is, they are a collective—a fully cohesive society."

"You're telling me that Marconi and the Wright brothers spoke to aliens?"

El grinned. "Heavens, no. As brilliant as those men were, they weren't ready. Even Moses had to view them through a holographic light wave transmission, which he, out of ignorance, called a burning bush. The Guardians don't need to reveal themselves to teach us. They have their means of feeding our minds. It's fascinating, really, a technologically produced telepathy. Think of it as a mental download. They'll seed a half dozen people at the same time with the same revelation, and let them compete to come out first with the invention—much the same way a farmer will overplant his field to ensure a bountiful harvest."

I didn't know what to say.

"Alan, I know this is difficult for you to accept. Changing a paradigm is never easy. But think about it. There is nothing more globally ubiquitous than the belief in extraterrestrial existence. The president of Russia spoke of aliens living among us, President Kennedy was caught on tape talking about secret alien captures, even Jimmy Carter publicly claimed to have seen a flying saucer. What surprises me is that you, or anyone else, would be surprised. Or, in this age of 'reason,' insist on living in denial.

"It is, perhaps, the only common ground that religionists and scientists share, both fighting to defend the indefensible argument that we are alone in the universe. And why? Because they don't want to know the truth."

"Why wouldn't they want to know the truth?" I said. "It's in their best interest."

El laughed. "Is it? Forgive my amusement, but for an advertising man you have a poor understanding of the human mind, Alan. People have always preferred mystery to truth. Most people don't even know the truth of their own beliefs. Ask them about the inner workings of their own religion or their religion's history and they pull their heads in like turtles. It's understandable. Religion is like sausage—it's best not to know what goes into it." He laughed again. "But there are those who are not afraid of the truth. People like you and me. It is our obligation and burden to act as shepherds to guide the flock."

Just then, the blue-haired man brought out our dinner. Sliced turkey breast, cranberry sauce, and mashed potatoes and gravy. I was as glad for the distraction as I was for the food.

"Ah, time to eat," El said.

"Looks like Thanksgiving dinner," I said.

"We *are* thankful," El said. "Our path is the way of gratitude. Please, allow me to give thanks for this food."

He raised his hands above his head and said in a loud voice, "Our God, who looks favorably upon thy chosen vessels, we praise Thee for thy goodness and power and our knowledge of Thee, the only truth, the only way, the only salvation. In the name of He who is worthy of worship throughout the universe, Jesus *the* Christ, Amen."

A chorus of "amens" filled the room. El looked at me. "Please, partake. The food is delicious. DarEl was a chef at the Four Seasons New York before he was enlightened."

El was right, about the food at least. Everything was exceptional. Thankfully, my host allowed me a moment to eat in silence. As I ate, I observed what was going on around the room. There was a bank of tables near one side where a dozen or more people were sitting with headphones on. There were others reading, all from the same book, a hardcover volume with a bright red and gold cover. A few others were cleaning. Everyone was busy.

A few minutes later I pointed to the group of people with headphones. "What are they listening to?"

El turned around to look at them. "Sermons. They listen for three to four hours a day. Usually after they finish their chores."

"Whose sermons?"

"Mine, of course."

"And the red books?"

"The Celestial Scripture. Prophecies I've received, including those of the last days before Christ returns and the earth receives its nuclear baptism of fire."

"Then you believe Christ will return?"

"Of course we do. And what a sight it will be, when

legions of crafts in the thousands and tens of thousands descend upon the earth, ushering in a new age of power and glory. The AhnEl will be there to assist in the transference of that power. Then we will be called up to our rightful place, and the kings and queens of this earth will be as our servants and our enemies will be as dust."

I gestured to the people in the room. "These people?"

"They shall rule the world."

"Where are they from?"

"The earth, of course."

"I assumed that."

"Assume nothing," El said. "They are the children of light. They are like the first stars in the twilight sky before nighttime is upon us and the fullness of the galaxy is seen in all its brilliance. But these are only a few of the enlightened. I have thousands of followers, in dozens of countries. I have nearly a hundred ordained missionaries out gathering the pure in heart, those not so darkened by their lusts and fears to hear truth. They are out seeking the tinder that is ready for the spark of enlightenment to blaze in their hearts and souls."

"These followers will do whatever you say?"

"I am their teacher and representative to the Guardians. Though, truthfully, I am merely a substitute teacher, filling in until the real teachers arrive—the Gods hasten that day! They could step in anytime. They are all around us. They have been for millennia."

"Your followers seem . . ." I hesitated.

El squinted. "They seem what?"

". . . Brainwashed."

His expression turned fierce. "Do you even know what that term means?"

"People whose brains have been coercively washed clean by some outside force," I said.

". . . And filled by another? Or should I say, programmed by another. You, of all people, should not be casting stones," he said, his voice ripe with disgust. "An *advertising* man."

"Our job was to inform," I said.

He laughed. "Is that what you told yourself?" He leaned on one elbow. "Your job was to change behavior to profit your clients. Am I right?"

"Yes," I relented.

"My motives are much more pure. I'm informing these people of the truth and providing them a practical structure in which the truth can flourish. Tell me, do these people look unhappy?"

I had to admit that they looked content. "No."

"Their service to me, is it beneath them?"

"Some would say—"

He pounded his fist on the table. "Don't patronize me. I'm not talking about some ambiguous cultural psychobabble. What do *you* say, Alan?"

His sudden outburst unnerved me. "Making others serve you seems self-serving."

He looked at me for a moment, then said with a softer voice, "Fair enough. But it is in losing themselves that they find themselves. It is in their service that they find use and meaning. Do you think they are suffering?"

"I don't know."

He tilted his head. "Then why don't you ask them? AshEl," he said, motioning over a young, strawberry-blond woman. She walked over to us, knelt at El's feet and kissed them. "Yes, Master."

"This Earthman wants to know if you are suffering."

"Suffering?"

"Yes, he's afraid you might be suffering here," he said. "You may speak to him."

She looked at me with a vacant expression. "Why would you think I'm suffering? Outside these walls the world is full of confusion and hate. For the first time in my life I feel peace." She turned back to El. "My master is to be praised for my salvation."

"Tell the Earthman about your life in the dark."

"I was an exotic dancer and an alcoholic. For the first time in my life I'm free." She again kissed El's feet.

He ran his hand over the crown of her head. "Thank you, AshEl. You may wait for me in my pod."

A large smile crossed her face. "Yes, Master. Thank you, Master."

She glanced back at me, then ran off.

"Suffering?" El said. "She's never been happier."

"What about the woman I met by the road?"

"Her sanctification is the most important thing she's done in her previously inconsequential life, as it is for all of them. I take their mental and spiritual anarchy and organize it, even as the Gods organized the chaos of space into this world and universe. I'm giving them order. And with it, joy, freedom and peace."

"I can see peace," I said, "maybe even a sense of happiness, but freedom?"

"Definitely freedom. Freedom from the burden of choice. The human mind, cynical as it may be, is seeking to be controlled. And, when you understand the mechanics of the human brain as the Guardians do, it is a very easy thing to control. Even one as intelligent as yours."

I said nothing and he looked at me with a dark, wry stare. "Well done, Alan. You're as wise as I thought."

"Why do you say that?"

"You didn't say that you couldn't be controlled. Ironically, the most susceptible to mind control are precisely those who don't believe they are susceptible."

My head was hurting. "Are you saying that your followers will do anything you say?"

He looked at me for a moment, then said, "Anything and *everything*. As they should."

"Would they kill for you?" I immediately regretted asking the question, realizing that I might have endangered myself.

His eyes turned dark. "I would not ask." Then, to my relief, his expression softened. "Enough of this. How was your dinner?"

I breathed out. "It was good."

"It was *exquisite*," he said. "I am fatigued. Do you have any other questions?"

"Just one. Do you believe in the devil?"

"Of course. But, again, we actually understand him. Actually, *them*. Like God, Satan is a group. More of a movement, a faction if you will."

"Explain," I said.

"The Guardians are democratic. They support the Father, Alpha and Omega, as their Supreme Leader. But, in all societies, there are dissenters. Especially when it comes to the issue of homo sapiens. The Guardian Supreme, or Godhead, believes that mankind has intrinsic value. They believe, if you will, in our potential. But not all of the Ahn are of the same opinion. Many, especially the Satanists, believe that humans are beasts, only good for servitude. They believe that too much knowledge has been given to humans already, wasted on us. They, like the Guardians, have access to the same telepathic technology. They use it to tempt us to defy the Guardians and to follow our baser, animal instincts, proving that we are, truly, primitive beings—something not easily disputable given the current state of humanity."

"Tempt?"

"Yes, temptation. Think of how inspiration works. It is simply the enlightening of the mind with an idea. Isn't temptation just inspiration with a negative bend?

"We are living in a spiritual war zone, Alan. Deny it at your own peril. Let he who has eyes see, the war rages on and soon everyone must choose a side. Freedom or eternal bondage. That is the only question. So let me ask you, Alan. Which side are you on? Will you join us? Or will you continue to wander, as you have, lost in a dark, confused world?"

"You're asking me to stay?"

"I'm *inviting* you to stay. At least for the night."

I hesitated. "I don't think so."

"Come on, Alan. Where will you go tonight? Sleep in the woods somewhere? It's late."

I looked around, weighing my options, not sure that I had any. I still wasn't sure what El was capable of and I was definitely outnumbered. If I needed to escape, it would be better at night. "All right," I said.

El tapped his glass with his fork and the blue-haired man appeared. "DarEl, please show Mr. Alan to a suitable pod. Show him the restroom facilities as well."

"Yes, Master."

"Thank you for dinner," I said to the young man.

"It was my pleasure," El replied. "A most enjoyable conversation."

✳

DarEl showed me to the bathroom, which was unisex with no stalls and no locking door, then he took me to a "pod," as they called it, a small bunkroom with six beds, just off the main room where we had dined. I claimed a bottom bunk and slid my pack under the bed. I didn't sleep. Even though El hadn't threatened me, I still felt like a prisoner. The entire experience was surreal. I wondered if this was how all of El's followers had begun. Had they initially been as skeptical as I was? Frankly, I was terrified. I knew that I had to get out of there.

Five others came into the room during the night and fell asleep. I just lay there quietly, waiting for something to happen. I wasn't disappointed.

CHAPTER

Thirty-one

The shackles of belief, when
reinforced by fear, are difficult to
break free from and rarely done.

Alan Christoffersen's diary

The sound I heard was a strained, painful whimpering, like the muffled cry of a wounded animal. I checked my watch. It was three thirty-six in the morning. No one in the pod stirred. I reached into my pack and felt for my gun. I didn't take it out, I was just reassuring myself of its presence. Then I got out of bed and crept to the door and looked out.

It was dark in the main room, illuminated only by the moonlight through the windows. In the far corner, near the audio tables, a woman was kneeling on the ground. Her hands were clasped around the back of her neck and her forehead was pressed to the rug. I looked around to make sure we were alone, then stole out, crossing the room. I knelt down next to her.

"Are you okay?" I whispered.

She jumped, startled by my voice, but, like the woman tied to the tree, didn't answer.

"What are you doing?" I asked.

She hesitated again, then, with her face still to the ground, whispered, "I'm being punished."

"Why?"

"I shouldn't be talking to you."

"It's okay."

For a moment she lay there, struggling with what to do. Then she looked up at me. She was young, probably not even twenty. She had short, sandy brown hair and dark brown eyes, large with fear. "Who are you?"

"You can trust me," I said.

She swallowed. "I asked to see my sister. I shouldn't have asked. So I'm being punished."

"Why can't you see your sister?"

"She's not a believer. It's for my own good."

"No it's not," I said. I put my hand on her back and she flinched. I looked to where her blouse was raised over her waist. There were red welts. "They did this to you?"

"I deserved my punishment."

"You need to get out of here," I said.

"I can't," she said. "Master El said I can't leave."

"I'll get you out of here."

She hesitated for a moment, then looked into my eyes. "You will?"

"Yes. But we have to leave now."

"The gate is guarded."

"We'll get out," I said. "Come on."

We silently crept back to my room. I took the gun out of my pack, checked the safety, then shoved a magazine into it and put it in my trousers. Then I put on my pack. The young woman sat on the floor next to me, shaking with fear.

"What's your name?" I whispered.

"EmEl."

"What's your real name?"

"My real name?"

"Your earth name," I said.

She hesitated and I wasn't sure if she'd forgotten it or was afraid to say it. "Emily," she said slowly, breathing out. "It's been a while since I've said that name."

"I'm Alan. Just do what I say and stay close to me."

We crouched down next to the door until I was sure no one was awake, then we crossed the main room to the entrance I'd come in through. I turned to Emily. "Is there an alarm?"

"I don't know."

"Be ready to run." I unbolted the door, then slowly opened it. Nothing. We quickly slipped out and I shut the door behind us. About five yards from the door we must have tripped a motion detector as several floodlights turned on.

"Hurry," I said, taking her hand. The gate was closed and we ran to the guard booth. A man was standing inside reading the red book. There was a red button on the wall next to him.

"Open the gate," I said.

My voice startled him. "What are you—"

"Open the gate," I repeated.

"I can't do that. Not without Master's permission."

I took out my gun and leveled it at him. "Then we'll do it ourselves. Step away from the button."

He still didn't move.

"You're illegally keeping us here. I'm within my rights to shoot you and open it myself. Either open it now or raise your hands and step back. Don't make me shoot you."

He hesitated just a moment, then raised his hands above his head and stepped back.

"Emily, push the button."

She looked at the man fearfully.

"If he touches you, I'll shoot him."

The man raised his hands higher. "I won't touch her. Please don't shoot me."

Emily stepped past him and pushed the button. There was a mechanical click and the gate began to open.

"I'm sorry, BarEl," she said to the man.

"Don't follow us," I said. "And don't sound an alarm."

The man swallowed but didn't move, paralyzed by fear. "It's no use running," he said. "The Guardians will find you."

"I'll take my chances," I replied.

⁎

I took Emily's hand and we ran out the gate, following the dirt road El and I had driven in on. The moon lit our path and I kept us moving at a brisk pace. Emily was struggling to walk and, even with my pack, I was faster than she was. We had gone about two hundred yards when she asked to rest.

"Are you okay?" I asked.

She was breathing heavily but nodded. A flood of lights turned on at the compound.

"We've got to hurry," I said. I grabbed her hand again and we ran as fast as we could.

Emily kept looking back. "They're coming!" she said.

I turned to see car lights coming up the road.

"This way," I said. I took her hand, and we ran off the road into the trees. Fortunately the entire drive was lined with forest. We went about twenty feet into the woods, until I was confident that we were invisible in the shadows, and squatted down. I took off my pack and checked my gun, then just sat on my haunches, waiting.

About two minutes later a minivan caught up to where we'd left the road. It was moving slowly, maybe five miles an hour. The passengers in the car had utility flashlights and were panning them around on both sides of the road.

"Stay low," I whispered.

Emily began to whimper.

I put my arm around her. "Everything will be okay. But I need you to be really quiet right now."

She nodded, even though her entire body was shaking with fear.

I was pretty keyed up as well. I didn't know what these guys were capable of, but from what I'd seen, likely anything El told them to do. I was sure of what I was capable of. If they came at us, I would shoot them. I'd been attacked before, and I wasn't going to let it happen again. And this time I had someone else to protect. I hoped it didn't come to that.

The car drove on past us until the red glow of their tail lights disappeared from our view. I figured we were still at least a mile from the main road. If they didn't come back, I'd have to assume they were watching the road and we'd have to hike through the forest to the highway. I wondered if they would be waiting for us.

"What do we do?" Emily asked.

"We just wait," I said. "They won't find us. Not here."

We sat there for about a half hour. The car never returned. Emily cradled her knees with her arms and rocked back and forth nervously.

"Are you okay?" I asked.

She looked pale. "BarEl was right. The Guardians can find us. They can track our DNA from space."

"El told you that?"

She nodded.

"Have you ever seen the Guardians?" I asked.

"No. But Master El has."

"No he hasn't," I said.

Ten minutes later I said, "Wait here." I crept out to the edge of the trees. Nothing. It occurred to me that they might not be looking for us at all, but may have just gone for the woman tied to the tree. That would make sense. Especially since BarEl had probably told them I had a gun. I went back to Emily. "They're gone. Are you tired?"

She nodded.

"We should get some sleep," I said. "Then start out in the morning."

"Okay," she said.

"How is your back?" I asked.

"It's okay."

"Really?"

"It kind of hurts."

"I have something for it." I took my hygiene bag out of my backpack and brought out a tube of Neosporin. "Let me put this on you."

She turned away from me and lifted her shirt. I gently rubbed the salve across her welts. When I was done, I put the ointment away and she turned back to me. She still looked scared.

"I have a phone," I said. I pulled it out of my pack and turned it on. "We can call your sister."

Emily didn't respond.

"What's her number?" I asked.

She just sat there staring at the phone, as if she were afraid of it. "In the morning," she said. "I'll call in the morning."

"Okay," I said. "Then let's get some sleep." I put the phone back in my pack, then led her deeper into the forest. I unpacked my tarp and mat and laid them both out behind a thicket of scrub oak. I brought out my sleeping bag and laid it over the tarp. "You can use my sleeping bag," I said.

"What about you?"

"I'm okay. I've got the mat and my coat."

She took off her shoes, then climbed into the bag.

I lay down on the ground with my head against my pack. "Emily, how did you get involved with this group?"

"I met a boy at a dance club."

"He was a member?"

"Yes. He was really sweet."

"Where is he now?"

"He's a missionary. So I don't see him."

"Did he bring other girls here?"

She didn't answer.

"Were you lonely?"

"Yes." I could hear her softly crying. After a moment she said, "Alan?"

"Yes?"

"What if Master El's right?"

"He's not."

"But how do you know? He said someone would come and try to take me away. And you came."

"Every cult says that," I said. "The first rule of a cult is to make you afraid of the rest of the world. Do you think that's what God wants? To make you hate the rest of His children?"

"But God's angry at us."

"Why is He angry at us?"

"Because we don't do what He tells us to do. He hates us."

"If you had a child, would you hate her because she

didn't always do the right things?" When she didn't answer, I said, "No, you wouldn't. You'd love her. And because you're an adult, you'd understand her mistakes and want to help her, for her good. That's who God is. If He made us flawed just to condemn us, what does that say about Him?"

She looked even more distressed. After a minute she said, "I have a child."

I looked at her. "Where?"

"My sister has her."

"You need to go back to her."

"KarEl won't love me with a child."

"Is KarEl the boy who recruited you?"

"Yes."

"He didn't really love you," I said. "He had an ulterior motive."

She sobbed softly for a few minutes. When she finally stopped, she said, "I've made a mistake."

"We all make mistakes," I said. "Everything will be okay. I promise."

After a moment she said, "Thank you."

"You're welcome. Now let's get some sleep."

She lay back and closed her eyes. I watched her for a few minutes, then rolled back over and fell asleep.

✦

It was late morning when I woke. My head ached, and I felt drained from the night before. The sound of insects filled the humid, morning air. But that's all I heard. I bolted up. Emily was gone. I looked around. There was no sign of her anywhere. She had gone back.

I remembered her words from the night, "I've made a

mistake." I completely misunderstood her. How stupid could I be?

I folded up my tarp and sleeping bag and stowed them in my pack, then, holding my gun, walked down the road back out to Highway 31. When I got to the highway, I returned my gun to my pack. No one was there.

CHAPTER

Thirty-two

Sometimes we can only find
ourselves by first losing ourselves.

Alan Christoffersen's diary

My next stop, in Prattville, was eighteen miles away. For the first few hours I was anxious that El might send someone after me and, as traffic was light along this section of highway, the sound of each approaching car filled me with trepidation. But nothing ever happened.

All day long I thought about Emily. I couldn't get the fearful look in her eyes out of my mind. I wondered what El would do to her once she returned. I should have been smarter. I had underestimated the pull the cult had on her and the thickness of those chains of fear and belief. I should have made her call her sister. I should have known that she might go back. What if she had been my daughter or sister or wife? What if she was Falene? Would I go back then? Of course I would. I felt guilty for failing her and cowardly for leaving her now. I might have been her only chance for freedom.

Spurred on by my anxiety and anger, I made good time, stopping only a few minutes for lunch by the side of the road. I reached Prattville by 5 P.M. and ate dinner at Fat Boy's Bar-B-Que Ranch on 1st Street. For the first time in years, I drank too much beer. Then I booked a room at the Days Inn on Main Street and went to bed early.

❈

The next morning I woke feeling hungover. I felt even worse emotionally. I felt guilty and lonely. I dialed information and was connected to the Alabama office of the FBI. I spent about forty-five minutes telling an agent about my experience with the cult and Emily. Though the agent seemed genuinely sympathetic, he warned me that cases like this generally didn't turn out well.

"The victims rarely cooperate against the group or its leader," he said. "And it's nearly impossible to prove someone's being held against their will if they're unwilling to leave." He added wryly, "If psychological manipulation was a crime, my wife would be on death row."

Still, he agreed to look into the group. I gave him my phone number and hung up.

Montgomery was only thirteen miles from Prattville, and I reached it before noon. I stopped for lunch, but no longer. Montgomery is a beautiful town with a rich history, but I had no desire to stick around and see the sights. I'm not sure why. Perhaps it was the darkness I'd carried with me since leaving the cult. Or maybe it was just that after walking more than twenty-five hundred miles, I was just a few weeks from Florida. I suppose the closer the magnet is to steel the stronger the attraction.

At lunch I casually glanced over my map, then, for the first and only time on my walk, I started off in the wrong direction. Instead of traveling east on Highway 82, I went south on 53. I had walked nearly three hours before I realized my mistake. Had I been in a car, I would have just turned around—but I wasn't in a car and miles, on foot, are hard-earned. After looking at my map again, I decided to continue on the route I'd taken, placating my mistake with fatalism: *maybe there was a reason I'd gone this way.*

Over the next five days my improvised route took me through a series of quiet, meandering roads—many through quiet little neighborhoods—south to Orion, then east at Troy to Clayton and Eufala before reconnecting with Interstate 82. In the end, I probably would have saved miles if I had just walked back to 82, but the road I'd chosen was worth the extra steps. The towns and suburbs I passed through fulfilled my expectations of a South I had hoped to find—a place still slow and rich, with southern drawls as thick as praline, faded Coca-Cola signs, and hand-drawn placards advertising homemade pecan brittle and boiled peanuts.

On one of those long stretches I remembered something Falene had said to me a few months after coming to work at the agency. We were pulling an all-nighter on a campaign for a brand of clothing called *Mason-Dixon.* Falene's job was to keep us swimming in coffee. It was probably three or four in the morning, and we were getting pretty punchy when she said to me, "I should have been born a southern girl."

"Why's that?" I asked.

"Because I'm a *rebel.*"

Maybe it was the hour, but I laughed for several minutes.

Thirty-nine days and seven hundred miles from St. Louis, I crossed the Chattahoochee River at Eufala into Georgia.

I walked twenty-three miles along the Jefferson Davis Memorial Highway and camped for the night just a mile west of Cuthbert. I was in a dark mood, and it wasn't until I was making camp that I realized why. It was the one-year anniversary of McKale's death.

CHAPTER

Thirty-three

I'm beginning to pick up the language down here. "Jeet?" means, "Have you eaten?" A "far truck" is useful in putting out "fars." "Bard" is past tense of borrow. There are four "tars" on a truck and "did" is the opposite of alive. Shopping carts are "buggies," buttons are "mashed" not pushed, and "Wal-Mart'n' " is a pleasant pastime.

Alan Christoffersen's diary

Cuthbert, Georgia, is famous for three past residents: former world heavyweight boxing champion Larry Holmes, former NFL defensive lineman Rosey Grier (who went on to work as a bodyguard for Robert F. Kennedy and was responsible for subduing Kennedy's shooter, Sirhan Sirhan), and Lena Baker, the only woman ever executed in the Georgia electric chair. There's a story there.

Lena Baker, an African-American woman, was born in 1901 in a slave cabin to a family of sharecroppers. She spent her life in dire poverty. At the age of forty-four she was taking in laundry to help support her mother and three children when a local gristmill owner and heavy drinker named Ernest Knight broke his leg and hired Baker to care for him.

Soon after taking the job, Knight, twenty-three years older than Baker, began forcing himself on her. When she tried to flee, Knight locked her in his gristmill. Baker escaped but was tracked down by Knight, who beat her and threatened to kill her if she left again. After weeks of living as his slave, she decided she couldn't take it anymore and one night, when he came for her, they "tussled" over his pistol. A shot was fired and Knight fell dead.

Baker was brought to trial under Judge William "Two

Gun" Worrill, and it took the all-white jury less than a half hour to reach a verdict of murder. Baker was taken to Reidsville State Prison, where she was kept in the men's section until, less than a month later, she was executed in "Old Sparky," making her the only woman in Georgia to ever die in an electric chair. Her last words were, "What I done, I did in self-defense. God has forgiven me. I have nothing against anyone. I picked cotton for Mr. Pritchett, and he has been good to me. I am ready to go. I am ready to meet my God."

As I approached Cuthbert that morning, the city looked incapable of such a deed. It looked kind and welcoming and today I'm sure it is. Besides, I always liked a town where the first thing you see is a baseball field. I stopped for breakfast at the Ranch House Restaurant, drawn in by their advertised "Buffet Every Day."

Cuthbert is an old southern town and had survived the war with some of her colonial homes intact. The city center had a roundabout, a large clock tower, a tea parlor, and the not-so-vintage Dawg House, a hot dog emporium.

Leaving the town, I saw something I had never seen before, a billboard cautioning travelers of an approaching intersection.

Dangerous Intersection Ahead

There must have been more than a few accidents, because, in addition to the billboard, I passed four more warning signs, three with flashing lights, all contributing to my general excitement to cross the "intersection of doom."

To my dismay, the crossroad looked identical to any

other intersection. I walked through it without even stopping, wondering what all the excitement was about.

The road from Cuthbert took me along miles of pecan trees intermingled with fields of cotton. Shortly before noon I stopped at a lone, ramshackle roadside store called Bruce's Country Corner. An A-framed sign out front read:

Cooking Today:
Muscadine & Scuppernong Jelly

From what I could see, I was the store's only customer, so I lay my pack down on the open porch and walked inside. Just inside the door was a woman sitting near a cash register reading a romance novel. She looked up as I entered. "Mornin'."

"Good morning," I said. I glanced around a moment, then asked, "What is muscadine and scuppernog?"

"Scupper*nong*," she said. "They're grapes. They grow wild around here."

I surveyed the store, a long, narrow hall of a place stacked with jams, jellies and preserves, handmade wooden knick-knacks, pecans, pecan logs, pecan ice cream, and pecan candies.

"There's more in back," the woman said. She pointed toward a narrow door as her eyes returned to her book.

I went to explore. The items in the back room were as eclectic as those in the front: Christmas decorations, saddles, farm implements, hard candies, boiled peanuts, and, most peculiar, carved walrus tusks and whale teeth. I asked the woman about the latter and she said, "Once a year a man comes by and trades them for pecans."

She offered me a sample of pecan brittle that, in all

honesty, was the best I had ever had. I purchased a half pound, then, before leaving, doubled it.

✳

My afternoon walk was pleasant, made more so when a parade of antique and vintage cars drove past me. There were Model A's, Model T's, Studebakers, LaSalles, Thunderbirds, Cadillacs—eye candy, all of them. Most of the drivers were men my father's age or older.

I reached the town of Dawson around six. I learned something about myself in Dawson. Priding myself, as most Seattleites do, for being racially "color blind," I realized that it's easier when you're in the majority. This was the first town I'd walked through where I hadn't seen a single other white man. Outside of my foreign travels, for the first time in my life I truly felt like a minority.

I stopped at a gas station for bottled water and on the way out asked a man idling near the gas pumps in a Dodge pickup truck if he knew of a nearby hotel.

"You want the cheap one or the special one?" he asked.

"The cheap one," I replied.

"Hop in," he said. "I'll give you a ride."

I put my pack in the truck's bed and climbed inside.

As he pulled out of the station he asked, "Where you walking from?"

"Seattle."

He looked at me like I was pulling his leg. "You come all the way from Seattle?"

"Yes, sir."

"Why would you go and do a thing like that?"

I looked at him for a moment, then said, "I guess I was bored."

He laughed the rest of the way to the hotel, a Budget Inn, where he wished me well on my journey. I thanked him, retrieved my pack from the back of his truck, then went inside. The rooms were just $24.99, and I ate a dinner of a T-bone steak and halibut at the Main St. Steak & Seafood restaurant, then went back to my hotel and to bed.

It took me two days to reach my next destination, the town of Sylvester. Nuts are big business in Sylvester, and the town has proclaimed itself the Peanut Capital of the World, although it was pecan stores and brokerages that lined the main thoroughfare.

I ate dinner at a Pizza Hut and booked a room at the Worth Inn, a small hotel with Pepto-Bismol pink room doors. The hotel had a Laundromat and I spent most of the night eating pecan brittle while doing my laundry and reading from a paperback book someone had left in the laundry room, *The Secret Life of Bees* by author Sue Monk Kidd. I thought it curious that the abandoned book was autographed, until I read on the book's back flap that Sylvester was Kidd's hometown.

CHAPTER

Thirty-four

I'm not a fan of boiled peanuts.
Just because you can boil something
doesn't mean you should.

Alan Christoffersen's diary

The next day I passed through the tiny township of Poulan—a town famous for giving out speeding tickets. Poulan was followed by the peculiarly named town of Ty Ty, where, at a small grocery mart, I tried my first muscadine grape. A muscadine is larger than any grape I'd ever seen; in fact, it looked more like a small plum than a grape, but it didn't taste as good as either.

That evening I reached Tifton, a tidy town with all the amenities of home. I ate dinner at the Hog-N-Bones Bar-B-Q & Breakfast and stayed at a Hilton Garden Inn. The hotel had a nice hot tub and swimming pool and I made good use of both.

I started the day with breakfast at the Waffle House. I decided that if I ended up going back to Seattle, I would think about buying a franchise. *Who doesn't like waffles?*

It was a hot day, and I stopped at noon for a swim in Hardy Creek, then walked on to a town called Enigma, where I stopped for lunch at the Corner Café. I thought the town's name curious, so I asked my server about it. Even though she didn't live in the town, it wasn't the first time she'd been asked and she was prepared.

Originally the town was called Gunn and Weston, until the city's founder, a man named John Ball, decided that wasn't a *real* name, so he presented two new names to state officials—Lax and Enigma. Astonishingly, Lax, Ball's first choice, was already taken, so the town was named Enigma. When he was asked why he chose the name Enigma, Ball replied, "I guess because it was a puzzle what to name it."

That night, as I began looking for a place to camp along the highway, I found an old, abandoned building hung with a faded sign:

C&C Woodcraft

The front door was slightly ajar, so I pulled it open and went inside. The building had a large front room with several smaller rooms in back. Surprisingly, the interior of the shop was partially intact, with hanging blinds, chairs and bookshelves. Most peculiarly, there was an upright piano in the corner.

The windows were almost all broken out and the place was full of garbage, which was true of *every* abandoned property I had passed through since Seattle. What it is that possesses people to throw garbage in these buildings I can't figure out. Were they just carrying their garbage around with them, saw a building and thought, *There's an old building. I think I'll throw my garbage in there!* Then again, back in Wyoming, people went out of their way to throw garbage into the beautiful Morning Glory Pool in Yellowstone National Park, so maybe people are just crazy with their garbage.

I cleared an area on the floor next to the piano, laid out my mat and sleeping bag and went to sleep.

✦

Physically, I was getting better. It had been more than a week since I'd had a headache of any concern and my legs and ankles didn't hurt anymore. I still tired more easily than I had pre-surgery, but even that was manageable. The next two days I averaged twenty-two miles and camped out both nights, nearly depleting my food and water. Fortunately, I was just a half day from the town of Waycross and the famous Okefenokee Swamp.

The swamp presented a problem. The Okefenokee is the largest "black water" swamp in North America, covering nearly a half million acres, or six hundred square miles. Waycross marked the beginning of the north border of the swamp and was the last major town along the highway until Folkston, which was more than thirty miles south. I wouldn't reach Waycross until noon. But even if I had started my day in town, I'd be hard-pressed to make Folkston by nightfall and I had no desire to camp outdoors near the critter-infested swamp. I would have to stop in Waycross and start early the next morning for one of the longest walking days of my entire journey.

I reached Waycross by twelve-thirty, booked a room at a Quality Inn, then walked to the neighboring Walmart for food, supplies and bug spray. I took everything back to my room, where I ate a club sandwich and Caesar salad for lunch.

✦

I hadn't always known that the Okefenokee Swamp was a real place. I first heard of the swamp from the Pogo cartoons my dad loved and in the contraband issues of *MAD* magazine I used to smuggle home and hide under my bed. (My mother said the magazine was "perverted" and banned me from reading it, which, of course, made it much more desirable. It wasn't until I was sixteen, eight years after my mother's death, that my dad found one of my hidden magazines. He picked it up, took it to his den and read it without saying a word. As it turned out, he had no objection to the magazine at all, which, for me, had two effects. First, it made me feel stupid for hiding them for all those years. And second, I lost interest in reading them.)

With a name as absurd-sounding as Okefenokee, I had always assumed that it was just a made-up place, like Shangri La or El Dorado. Okefenokee is a Native American Hitchiti tribe word meaning "shaking waters."

❖

With most of my day left, I had the hotel call a cab to take me the eight miles to the Okefenokee Swamp Park. The road from the park's entrance to the visitor center was five more miles. There were fewer than a dozen cars in the park's parking lot.

The visitor center had a gift shop featuring shelves of alligators, and alligator parts, fashioned into bizarre novelties: alligator-claw key rings, necklaces and back-scratchers; gator-skinned wallets, business card holders, and iPhone covers; lacquered alligator heads, stuffed baby alligators dressed as golfers or brides and grooms, and full-grown stuffed alligators guaranteed to keep the neighbors' dog off your lawn.

I signed up for a boat tour, which I was told would be departing in five minutes. I hurried to the boarding dock. There were already people in the boat, an elderly couple in the back row and a family in the front two rows: mother, father and two teenage boys. I took a seat in the center.

As we waited for our guide, the man sitting in front

of me turned around and said, "We're the Andersons. I'm Boyd and this is my wife, Dawn."

"Like the sunrise, not the Trump," Dawn said.

"Nice to meet you," I said. "I'm Alan Christoffersen."

"Where are you from, Alan?" she asked.

"Seattle."

"You're a long way from home," Boyd said. "Where are you headed?"

"Key West."

"So are we," Dawn said. "Maybe we'll run into you there."

"You'll probably be long gone by the time I get there," I said.

"Oh?" she replied. "Making other stops on the way?"

"I'm walking."

"You're walking from Seattle to Key West?" Boyd asked.

"Every step of the way," I said.

"Did I hear that right?" the elderly man behind me said. "You walked here all the way from Seattle?"

I turned around. "Yes."

"That's amazing," he said. "I've always wanted to walk across America and you've done it."

His wife looked at him quizzically. "You have?"

"I've thought about it many times."

"Probably just to get away from me," she said.

The man offered his hand. "Pleased to meet you. We're the Pitts of Montgomery, Alabama. I'm Eric and this is my beautiful wife, Peggy."

I shook her hand, then his. "It's a pleasure," I said. "I'm Alan Christoffersen. I walked through Montgomery a week or so ago."

"What did you think of it?" Peggy asked.

"It's a beautiful town," I said.

She smiled. "We're pleased you enjoyed it."

＊

Two men walked along the dock and one of them stepped off into the back of the boat, next to the outboard motor. He squeezed a black rubber priming ball, then pushed a button and the motor fired up, sputtering in the water behind us.

"Good afternoon, y'all." He was an older gentleman, maybe in his late sixties, thin, with a straw hat and an accent as thick as the swamp water. He wore denim jeans and a long-sleeved cotton shirt. "My name is Herman and I'd like to welcome y'all to the world-famous Okefenokee Swamp. Before we set sail, let me tell you a few things. In case we sink, the exit is all around you. Secondly, y'all will want to keep your hands inside the ride at all times. Some of the critters are always looking for a handout." He laughed at his rehearsed jokes, and we politely laughed.

Herman untied the boat and his helper shoved us off with his foot, then he put the boat in gear, driving us forward. Thirty feet ahead we passed under a walking bridge and the canal narrowed to about fifteen feet wide.

"If you fall in, it's not deep," Herman said. "But I wouldn't stay in too long."

"The water looks gross," one of the teenage boys said.

"Looks like beer," Eric said.

Herman took the boat out of gear, then reached a bucket over the side and scooped up a gallon of the water, tilting it slightly forward so we could see it. "You might think there'd be a lot of skeeters in this water but there ain't. That's because it's so filled with tannic acid, it kills them." He handed the bucket to Eric. "Here, y'all tell me if it tastes like beer."

Eric pursed his lips. "I'll pass, thank you."

"It stinks," Peggy said.

"That's methane gas," Herman said. "Same stuff cows emit from their backsides."

She grimaced and Herman laughed. "Every now and then somethin' will ignite the swamp gas and you'll hear an explosion out here like a shed o' dynamite." He put the motor back in gear and the boat plowed ahead.

"What kind of trees are these?" Peggy asked.

"These right here are cypress. I'll tell y'all somethin', these cypress trees can live up to six hundred years. Every inch of thickness equals twelve and a half years of growth. So, you can see, some of these trees are hundreds of years old.

"As you probably know, the swamp's full of all kind of critters. There are thirty-four different kinds of snakes in the swamp and I seen every one of 'em. Six of 'em are venomous, includin' the famous water moccasin, or cottonmouth, eastern diamondback rattler and the coral snake.

"We also got some fine specimen of spiders," he said to Dawn. "Like the one right above your head."

Dawn looked up and screamed. The spider was yellow and black and nearly the size of my hand. Its web spanned the width of the creek.

"Now watch this," our guide said. He grabbed a section of the web and plucked it like a banjo string. "Now that is strong! The government is studyin' this, tryin' to duplicate it. Inch per inch, this web is stronger than steel."

We were more intent on the massive spider hanging above us than its web, which, in spite of our guide's provocation, seemed content to stay where it was.

"If y'all look to the port side on the bank there, you'll see a big ol' hole with the brush all pushed back. That's an alligator nest. The gator there we call Miss Daisy and her eggs hatched just last week. We got a half dozen of her babies back at our center for their own protection. These baby gators get gobbled up by just about everythin' that can get to them, raccoons, birds and other gators.

"An interestin' fact about gators, the temperature determines their gender. During their incubation if the temperature averages above ninety-three degrees, they'll be male gators. If it's cooler than that, you got females. It's been hot lately, so this brood was all male."

The boat continued up the canal. Nailed to a tree overhanging the bank twenty yards ahead of us was a sign, printed backward and upside down. "Y'all might want to get a picture of this before our waves make it hard to see."

ⒾⒶKE
ⓂⒾⓇⓇOⓇ

The sign's reflection in the water read:

MIRROR
LAKE

The boat churned up the narrow black waterway for another five minutes before our guide started speaking again.

"That big ol' rusty kettle up on your left is a still. Back durin' Prohibition, the swamp was lit up like Christmas with all the stills pumping out illicit moonshine. We've got two kinds of stills in here, turpentine and whiskey. It's best not to get them mixed up, but sometimes there's not a whole lot of difference 'tween the two.

"This still right here was for alcohol. It was owned by a feller they called Lightnin' Larry. The locals gave his moonshine whiskey a special name: Autumn Leaves. Anyone wish to venture a guess why they called his brew Autumn Leaves?"

"Because he only made it in autumn," Peggy said.

"No," Herman said with a grin, "it's because you'd take one drink of the stuff, change colors and fall."

We all laughed.

"Now take a moment to notice some of the unique foliage around us. On your right is the pitcher plant. It's one of several carnivorous plants in the swamp, includin' the Venus flytrap. Even the plants in the swamp have a bite."

Our excursion lasted about forty-five minutes in all. We didn't encounter a single alligator, which was disappointing to me. After we had docked and tipped Herman, I walked around the park for a while, looking down from the boardwalk into wood-sided pens filled with alligators and snapping turtles, all of which looked more dead than alive.

A little more than an hour after I arrived, I returned through the visitor center, where I purchased a cold bottle of water and a Snickers bar. I had just stepped out onto the curb to call the cab company from my cell phone when a minivan pulled over in front of me. I walked up to the passenger-side window where Dawn sat.

"Sure you don't want a ride to Key West?" she said.

"We've got room," Boyd added, "if you don't mind sitting in back with the boys."

"Thank you, but no. I'm hoofing it."

"Then how about a lift to town?" Dawn said.

"I'll take you up on that," I replied.

"Brandon," Boyd said, "open the door."

The boy slid the side door open, and I climbed in, shutting the door behind me.

"Are you really going to walk all the way to Key West?" Brandon asked.

"I really am."

"You're nuts," he said.

"Brandon!" his mother said sternly.

"He's right," I said. "I am."

"What's that on your head?" the other boy, who looked a little older, asked from the back seat.

"Chris!" shouted Dawn. She turned to me. "I'm so sorry."

"It's okay," I said. I turned to Chris. "About three months ago I had a tumor about this size removed from my brain." I made a circle with my thumb and forefinger.

"Cancer?" Dawn asked.

"No. It was benign."

"What does that mean?" Brandon asked.

"It means it's not going to kill me," I said.

"Praise God," Dawn said.

"Does that have something to do with why you're walking?" Boyd asked.

I shook my head. "No. It just made it a little tougher."

After about ten minutes, Boyd rolled the van to a stop in front of my hotel. I slid open the door and climbed out. "Travel well," I said.

"You walk well," Boyd said.

"We'll warm up Key West for you," Dawn added.

"Thanks. Have a good time." I pointed at the two boys. "Especially you two."

They were both playing video games on their phones and just kind of nodded. I shut the door and Boyd turned back to the highway. I ate dinner at the El Potro Mexican Restaurant, then went to bed early.

I didn't sleep well. Mexican food isn't the best choice for a good night's rest, and I was nervous about the upcoming stretch. It had been a while since I'd walked more than thirty miles in one day and that was before my craniotomy. *Don't worry, you'll make it,* I told myself. *You always do.*

CHAPTER

Thirty-five

Some so fear the future that they
suffocate the present. It's like committing
suicide to avoid being murdered.

Alan Christoffersen's diary

My alarm rang at five-fifteen. Getting up before the sun wasn't as easy as it had been in times past. I didn't feel my best but convinced myself that it was just the early morning and I'd soon walk my way out of it. I packed and went down to the hotel lobby for breakfast. I had a couple of waffles, coffee and some scrambled eggs with chili sauce.

I asked the hotel clerk about the availability of rooms in Folkston. He named several hotels and assured me that they would have rooms available at this time of year. I finished my breakfast, then set out on Highway 23.

As any long-distance runner can attest, there are days when you feel light-footed as a gazelle—as if the law of gravity has been temporarily repealed and the ground itself seems to propel you. Then there are those days your feet feel like anvils. Unfortunately, this, of all days, was the latter.

After just three miles of walking, my pack felt heavier than it had in weeks, the road harder, my footwear less comfortable and my balance less keen.

I doubted my physical state was a coincidence and wondered if my body was rebelling because I was forcing it to do what it didn't want to do and probably shouldn't—walking a marathon *plus* a 10k, while still recovering from brain surgery and carrying fifty-plus pounds on my back. I felt like I was dragging myself every inch of the way.

Around noon I stopped along the side of the road to eat lunch, a somewhat smashed ham, turkey and cheese hoagie I had bought at Walmart the day before, an apple, string cheese and a Clif Bar, hoping the carbs might help my lagging energy. If they did, it wasn't noticeable.

I didn't stop long but doggedly trudged along the highway corridor—the swamp and railroad tracks to my right, thick brambles and forest to my left, a seemingly endless road in front of me. Around three in the afternoon I began doubting I was going to make it to Folkston. Around four I was almost certain of it and began telling myself that camping in the swamp might not be that bad after all. Truthfully, I didn't sound all that convincing, so I kept walking.

Around six o'clock I was practically staggering when a turquoise and beige Chevy pickup truck with two rifles visible through its back window pulled up to the side of the road about thirty yards ahead of me and turned on its hazard lights. The truck was far enough ahead that I wasn't sure if the driver had stopped on my account or for something else.

As I approached the vehicle, I casually looked over. "Evening."

The driver, a sixty-something balding man wearing a hunting jacket and Seminoles ball cap, said in a gruff voice, "You need a ride?"

The man looked like the sheriff from *Deliverance*.

"I'm not sure," I said. "How far are we from Folkston?"

"About twelve miles."

I thought I was closer. I didn't have twelve miles left in me. "Are you headed to Folkston?"

"No. I'm headed home. It's about a mile up ahead." He squinted. "Were you thinking of hoofing it to Folkston tonight?"

"I was planning to. But it's farther than I thought. I might just have to camp. I have a tent."

His brow furrowed. "You're in the swamp, son. A little nylon ain't worth nothing for protection. If the skeeters don't get you, there's the gators, rattlers, cottonmouths, panthers and bears. And if one of them don't, the moonshiners will. Somethin's always huntin' somethin' in the swamp.

"I've got a camping trailer at my place. Not air-conditioned or nothin', but it's comfortable and safe."

I thought about it for a moment, then said, "All right. Thank you."

"Just put your pack in the back."

I slid off my pack and heaved it over the side of the truck's bed, then opened the door and climbed in the front seat. The seat was dusty and there were crushed beer cans on the floor.

"Just kick' em out of the way," he said. He turned off his hazards, then put his truck in gear and we lurched forward. When we were up to speed, he said, "I'm Dustin."

"Alan," I said. "You've lived here your whole life?"

"Most of it. I was born in Tallahassee." He looked over. "Where are you from?"

"I was born in Colorado, but raised in Pasadena."

"California boy," he said somewhat disparagingly. "What part of Colorado?"

"Near Denver."

"I've got a cousin in Pueblo," he said. "Where are you walkin' from?"

"Seattle."

"Jiminy Christmas," he said. "You've walked that far?"

"Yes."

"You were plannin' on walkin' from Waycross to Folkston in one day?"

"I've walked that far before," I said. "But I had a brain tumor removed a few months back and I guess I'm not all the way back up to speed."

"You stopped your walk to have a brain tumor removed, then came back out?"

"Yes."

He smiled. "You're a manly man." We drove a minute in silence, then he said, "See any gators on the highway?"

"No. Do they ever come out that far?"

He smiled. "Oh, they're there. People usually just mistake them for old tires."

I had actually wondered why so many people had thrown out their tires along this stretch of road. I realized I had probably walked by more than a dozen of them without even knowing it.

"Do you know where alligators got their name?"

I shook my head. "Never thought about it."

"The first explorers in Florida, the Spaniards, called them El Lagarto. Sounds like al-li-gator. *Lagarto* means 'lizard' in Spanish."

"Big lizards," I said.

"I've seen plenty of big ones," he said. "You have to just assume that any body of water around here has a gator in it. Had a real tragedy a couple years back, a mother left her four-year-old son on a picnic blanket while she ran just ten yards to get something out of the car. She wasn't gone thirty seconds, but when she turned around, all she saw was her son missin' and the tail of the gator goin' into the water."

"That's horrific," I said.

"Extremely horrific," he said.

We drove for what seemed several miles, farther than he said his place was, but then, at the first available turnaround, he pulled a U-turn and headed back a mile or so before turning east off the highway. We drove up a forest-lined dirt road for about a quarter mile before we reached his property, crossing two creeks over wooden bridges made with railroad ties.

An eight-foot-tall chain-link fence topped with barbwire surrounded his place and the opening gate was locked and chained. It reminded me a little of the AhnEl cult's compound, though much humbler and not nearly as orderly or clean.

At the entrance, Dustin pulled a large ring of keys from his ignition, then got out of the truck, unlocked the padlock, then unwound the chain that held the gates together. He dragged open the gate and we drove inside.

The home was maybe 1,500 square feet and had barred windows and concrete walls with a forest green corrugated tin roof that had been enhanced with flourishes of spray-painted camouflage. Connected to the home was a propane tank covered with a steel grate.

Partially visible near the back of the house was a wooden storage shed and to the side of the house was an eighteen-foot-high carport, which covered two ATVs and an older model twenty-six foot Winnebago RV. There was also a Fleetwood camping trailer.

The place looked a little like an automobile graveyard, with an assortment of vehicles scattered around the yard. In addition to the RVs, there were two and a half trucks in disrepair, an old station wagon up on blocks and an aged

yellow Caterpillar wheel-loader tractor that looked powerful enough to clear forests.

He parked the truck next to the house and we
climbed out.

"You can stay in the Winnebago over here," he said,
nodding toward the RV. "It's the most comfortable."

"Thanks," I said.

I grabbed my pack and we walked over to the trailer.
He again took out the massive ring of keys and opened
the door. We both went inside.

"The big bed's just at the end of the hall. You can use
the toilet if you want. I'll turn the pump on."

"This looks really comfortable," I said.

"Better than sleeping with the gators," he said.

I lay my pack down on a bench in the kitchen.

"Have you had dinner?" Dustin asked.

"No, not yet."

"You carryin' it in your pack?"

I nodded. "As usual."

"I'm makin' stew. It's been in the Crock-Pot all day. You
can join me if you like."

"That sounds better than anything in my pack. I'm
pretty hungry."

"Let's eat."

I followed him back out of the RV. The sun was beginning to set and the yard was already obscured with
shadow. "Come into the house."

I followed him inside. His front door was thick metal
with two deadbolts and set in a metal frame.

"How long have you lived back here?" I asked.

"Five years. It's my ark."

"Ark?"

"Like Noah," he said. "When the rains come, I'll be ready."

I walked into the front room. Dustin was clearly a hoarder, and all the countertops, shelves and chairs were piled high with clutter.

Against the one windowless wall was an ancient console television. On top of it was a ham radio and a 12-gauge shotgun shell press filled with buckshot. On the carpeted floor below it were tubes of black powder and empty casings.

On the other side of the console were several framed pictures—one a family portrait with a younger Dustin standing next to a woman and a teenage boy and girl. The other two pictures were of the same woman, though in one of the pictures she looked twenty years younger than the other.

"Is this your family?" I asked.

I noticed his expression fall a little. "Yeah. Just a minute." He walked out of the room, returning a few minutes later carrying a loaf of white bread. Then he took two bowls from a cupboard above the stove. He set them on the counter next to the Crock-Pot and dished out two heaping ladles of stew into each. He carried them over to an oblong wood dining table, which divided the front room from the kitchen.

"Supper's ready," he said.

I walked over and sat down while he grabbed some spoons, two blue enamel cups and the bread. He sat back down, tore off the end of the loaf and handed it to me with my bowl.

"The stew's hot," he said.

I lifted a spoonful, blowing on it before putting it in my mouth. It was surprisingly good.

"You're a chef," I said. "What kind of meat is this?"

"Venison. I know it don't taste like it, that's because I let it stew all day. Takes the gaminess out of it."

He took a piece of bread and scooped up some of the stew. "With that brain tumor did you have to go on chemo or anythin'?"

"No. It was benign. And they were able to cut it all out."

"You're lucky," he said.

"I am."

When I finished the bowl, he asked if I wanted more.

"Please," I said. "If there's enough."

"I made plenty," he said. "I usually make enough for three or four days. It freezes well."

As I finished my second bowl, Dustin said, "I suppose walkin' like you do, you can eat a lot."

"That's true. I figure I burn five-to-six thousand calories a day."

He nodded. "Want more?"

"No. Two bowls is plenty. It's good, though. Thank you."

"Glad you liked it." He reached across the table and took my bowl, then grabbed his own and carried them to the sink. He came back a minute later and tossed a couple packages of Twinkies on the table. "Like Twinkies?" he asked.

"Who doesn't?"

"They last forever," he said.

The Twinkie actually looked good. As I tore back the cellophane wrapper, he stooped down into a cupboard and brought out a large jug filled with a clear liquid.

"You drink?" he asked.

"On occasion," I said.

"I've got a still out back, makes some of the best rotgut in these parts. Pour you a swig?"

"Sure," I said. I had always wondered what moonshine tasted like.

He poured the two cups halfway. He took a short drink, then looked at me, waiting for me to follow. Ignoring the smell, I took a drink. It was like swallowing rubbing alcohol and burned my throat. I gagged, then coughed loudly, which made Dustin laugh.

"Got a little kick to it," he said.

"Shotguns have less kick," I said. "Are you sure that's not turpentine?"

My question pleased him. "Oh it's moonshine all right," he said. "Made from corn mash. Distilled it myself. Not for the faint of heart."

"I guess I'm fainter of heart than I realized." I tried a little more, but it wasn't for me. With a condescending look he reached across the table and took my cup and downed it. He didn't cough, but his face turned red.

"It's an acquired taste," I said.

"Not for the faint of heart," he said again. A minute later he asked, "Why are you walkin'? You're not runnin' from the law, are you?"

"With all the guns you have around here, do you think I'd tell you if I was?"

He laughed. "Not if you're smart."

"No, I didn't do anything criminal. I started walking because my wife died."

His countenance immediately changed. "I'm sorry. How'd you lose her?"

"She was in a horse-riding accident. She broke her back."

He shook his head empathetically, then breathed out slowly. "I lost my wife too," he said.

"Is that her over there?" I said, pointing to the pictures on the console.

He nodded. "That's Janean." He looked down at his drink, then lifted it and took another swig. "You know what Janean means? It means 'God is gracious.'" His eyes moistened and I could tell that the moonshine was taking effect. "He was gracious with her, at least. She was everythin' a man could want."

"How did you lose her?"

"Wasn't a horse," he said. "A horse's ass, maybe." He sighed. "I dunno."

"You're divorced?"

"Not that I know of. I mean, who's going to serve me papers out here? They'd never be found again. Not that it matters. She's been gone for two and a half years."

"What happened?"

He took another drink before answering. "She didn't want the life out here. It's ironic, you know. I built this place to protect her from the world and keep *her* safe, and I lost her because of it. She said she was sick of living holed up like a badger. She said she was sick of livin' paranoid and if the world was goin' to end then she wanted to end with it, not go out fightin' it. She poisoned the kids against me." His demeanor turned angry. "I built this place for *their* good. When the world goes to hell, they'll be back." He nodded as if assuring himself. "They'll be back. They'll see I was right."

"What if it doesn't go to hell?" I asked.

"It will. It's just a matter of time before the whole house of cards comes fallin' down. This country's been movin' in the wrong direction a long time. It's just a matter of time."

"And if you're right, then what?"

"I'll be ready. It will take an entire army to get me out of here. I can blow the bridges on the way in. I've got an arsenal Bin Laden would've envied. I've got AK-47s, M-16s, shotguns, knives, machetes, dynamite, even a thousand gallons of gasoline under the house. You know what I've got? This will blow your mind. I've got a flame-thrower."

"Where'd you get a flame-thrower?"

"I made it myself from a book I found on the Web. Shoots a fifty-foot flame. I've also got MREs, and a five-thousand-gallon water tank filled by my own well."

"How do you think it will go down?" I asked. ". . . In the end."

"I don't know. I've thought through a couple dozen scenarios. You've got your world government, you've got terrorist groups with nuclear and chemical weapons, or, worse yet, EMPs. Do you know what EMPs are?"

"Electromagnetic pulse," I said.

"Do you realize how easily someone could take us out with an EMP? One EMP blast could fry all of the computers and wires within a thousand miles. Shut down entire cities, all commerce, all refrigeration, all transportation, all communication, all hospital machinery. Hundreds of thousands of people would die the first week.

"Then you've got your pandemics. Do you know how many people were killed by the Black Death? Half of Europe. And that was back when the world was isolated. Today a pandemic would kill more than three billion people. I know it sounds like movie stuff, but a couple years ago there was a super virus discovered in Israel. If it had gotten out of quarantine, they estimate it would have been worse than the Black Death. We're that kid with his finger in the dike, you know. It's just a matter of time before it goes."

I poured myself a little of the moonshine and this time forced it down without gagging.

"What do you think?" he asked.

"You probably don't want to know," I said.

"Try me," he said in a low voice.

I wiped my mouth, then looked up at Dustin. "I think if terrorists blow up our largest cities with nuclear weapons, we lose all power and a pandemic ravages what's left of the world while roving gangs prey off the weak, I'd just as soon not stick around for it. What's the worst thing that could happen to us? We die? We're all going to die."

"It's not just about you," Dustin said. "You could lose your loved ones."

I looked at him for a moment, then said, "Like you already did?"

He just stared at me for a moment, then, grabbing the jug, got up and went into the other room.

Stupid thing to say, I thought.

When I decided he wasn't coming back, I got up and went out to the Winnebago. I felt bad that I'd offended my host. He'd been kind to take me in. Still I locked the door and got my gun out. I didn't know what kind of a drinker Dustin was, and with the arsenal he had at his disposal, I feared him more than anything else in the swamp.

CHAPTER

Thirty-six

Why did the man cross America? To see
what was on the other side of himself.

Alan Christoffersen's diary

I woke early the next morning, packed up, then went over to Dustin's house and knocked on the door. His truck was still there, so I assumed he was too. After my third time knocking, I decided that he was probably still asleep or hungover from the moonshine he'd ingested the night before. I tore a page from my journal and left him a note thanking him for his hospitality, then set off for the day.

Physically, I felt much better than I had the day before, which made me believe my difficulty walking had been, at least in part, psychosomatic. It was an easy, brisk walk down the dirt road back to the highway, then only eleven miles south to the town of Folkston. I could have easily walked farther, but I didn't. My planned route into Florida went from Waycross to Folkston over the Florida border to Callahan, then southeast into Jacksonville. I wanted the crossing of my last state border to be more than an afternoon side note.

Four miles before Folkston, I passed a billboard that read:

Florida Lotto Tickets,
9 miles ahead.
Gas n' Go Boulogne

Florida. If you had asked me as I left Seattle if I would make it here, I would have shrugged. But I had. I was on my last lap, so to speak.

Like Waycross, Folkston also calls itself the "Gateway to the Okefenokee." I ate a buffet dinner at the Okefenokee Restaurant, with pork chops and popcorn shrimp, then found a room at a bed and breakfast called the Inn at Folkston, a quaint, restored 1920s heart-pine bungalow. McKale would have loved it.

The only room they had available was the English Garden Room—which is also their bridal suite—themed after an English country inn, with a large sitting area and a gas fireplace. The room was beautiful and reportedly inhabited by a ghost, but the only thing that haunted me that night was my thoughts.

Long into the night I lay there thinking. The next day I would cross into Florida. I was nearing the end of my walk. *Then what? Where was I going next? What would I do with the rest of my life?* In response, what kept playing through my mind was the last thing McKale said to me as she lay dying: "Live."

At that time, when I had no desire to go on, I had only considered that she had meant not taking my life. Now I realized that she had meant more than that. To truly live is more than taking the next breath—it's to hope and dream and love. That's what she really meant. She, who was my hope and dream and love, was telling me to go on without her.

Here, on the final stretch of my walk, I realized that what I wanted most *was love.* After all I had been through, I couldn't bear the idea of reaching Key West only to walk across the border without a single person to share it with. And that was true of the rest of my life. Why hadn't I understood this sooner?

Perhaps it was, like my father had said, as simple as a matter of faith. Faith that life could be worth living again after my love's death. Faith in life itself. Faith in love itself. I hadn't been willing to risk loving again, because I wasn't willing to risk losing again. I had feared the future so much that I was killing it.

I was not so different from Dustin, the man in the swamp. Fearing the future, he had isolated himself with fences and barbwire and guns, just as I had done emotionally. And the result was the same—we had both run love out of our lives.

Somewhere in the internal dialogue of that night, I confronted the truth about myself and, in so doing, found the courage to obey McKale's final request. I was ready to take a chance. I was ready to live again.

CHAPTER

Thirty-seven

A good read should introduce new
drama in each chapter. But that's
just in books. What may be enjoyable
in literature is not so in real life.

Alan Christoffersen's diary

The weather the next morning was as balmy as one expects of Florida. The weather in my heart was equally serene. I knew what I wanted. I wanted love in my life. I wanted Falene.

When I had read her letter on the plane, I was not just surprised by her feelings but by my own. I cared more deeply for her than I had ever allowed myself to admit. Now, in this new day, I was ready to face those feelings. I was going to see this through. I wasn't going to Key West without her. I was going to find Falene if I had to park a month in Jacksonville to do it, or visit every modeling agency in New York. As I thought about this, I felt something I hadn't felt in a very long time. I felt alive.

✳

Breakfasts at B&Bs are always good and the Inn at Folkston was no exception. I ate breakfast outside on the wood-planked patio. I had a stack of blueberry pancakes, honeydew melon, baked ham and "Chicken George's" fresh eggs.

The clear, warm air smelled of the sweet fragrance of tea olive and honeysuckle.

After breakfast I went back to my room to check my

cell phone. It had been a while since I'd turned it on and I wondered if Carroll had called.

I discovered that my phone was dead. I found the charger and plugged it into the wall. After about thirty seconds the phone turned on and immediately vibrated. I looked at its screen. I had eight missed calls and two voicemail messages. All of the calls were from the same two numbers. I didn't recognize either, but both had Pasadena area codes.

I played the first message.

"Alan, this is Carroll. Sorry it took so long but I found your friend. Her phone number is area code 212, 555–5374. Good luck."

My heart pounded. This was my miracle, wasn't it? An answer to my night's epiphany?

I played the message again and wrote down Falene's phone number on a piece of note paper next to the room's telephone. I nervously held the paper in one hand, my phone in the other, until I started laughing at myself. After all the time I'd known Falene, I was flat out terrified to call her. Where would I begin? What if she'd changed her mind about me? I felt as awkward as a teenager calling for a first date.

As I thought over what I would say, I looked back down at my phone. There was still the other message. I pushed play.

"Alan, this is Nicole. Please call as soon as you get this. It's an emergency."

Her voice was strained. *Why was she calling from Pasadena?* I dialed the number. It rang just twice before Nicole answered. "Alan?"

"Nicole? What's wrong?"

"You need to come home," she said.

"What's wrong?"

"Your father's had a heart attack."

For a moment I was speechless. "Is he still alive?"

"He's in intensive care."

"Is he going to make it?"

There was a long pause. Then she said, "You just need to come home."

EPILOGUE

Again, my world is in commotion. The
only thing that hasn't changed in my
life is the uncertainty of it all.

Alan Christoffersen's diary

I took a cab to the Jacksonville airport, just thirty-six miles from Folkston. *Just.* By foot that's two days of travel—by car it's less than an hour. By plane I'll have traveled as far as I've walked this last year before evening.

My flight to Los Angeles left Jacksonville at 5 P.M., with an hour layover in Atlanta. I never called Falene. There was already too much on my emotional plate.

I called Nicole from my layover to see if there were any changes in my father's condition, but she didn't answer. This intensified my fear. Did I regret not staying home with my father as he'd wanted me to? Of course I did. But I pushed the thought from my mind. Regret is a useless emotion: it's like brushing your teeth after you find a cavity.

As I write this, I am about twenty minutes from touchdown in Los Angeles. What am I going to find? My heart is a battleground of hope and fear, each, in turn, seizing control. I'm afraid of the news that will shortly come. I'm afraid that I may already be orphaned.

Honestly, I do not have faith that I will see my father again. But I have hope. I hope that my father is still alive and that he'll be okay. I hope that I can see him again and tell him everything that's in my heart. But most of all, if it is his time, I hope for the chance to be there for him as he always was for me. I don't know if God will grant me this. But I hope.

For now Key West must wait. For the third time since I began, my walk has been delayed. In the beginning, I had considered these stops on my journey as interruptions—but I'm coming to understand that perhaps these detours *are* my journey. No matter how much I, or the rest of humanity wishes otherwise, life is not lived in smooth, downhill expressways, but in the obscure, perilous trails and rocky back roads of life where we stumble and feel our way through the fog of the unknown. Life is not a sprint. It was never meant to be. It is just one step of faith after another.

To be continued.
Coming May 2014, Book 5 of
The Walk series.

Coming May 2014, book 5 of The Walk series

To learn more about The Walk series
or to join Richard's mailing list and
receive special offers and information, please visit:
www.richardpaulevans.com

Join Richard on Facebook at the
Richard Paul Evans fan page
www.facebook.com/RPEfans

Or write to him at:
P.O. Box 712137 • Salt Lake City, Utah • 84171

SIMON & SCHUSTER
READING GROUP GUIDE

A STEP OF

RICHARD PAUL EVANS

INTRODUCTION

Alan Christofferson is a broken man. Following the sudden death of his wife and the betrayal of his former business partner, the once-successful advertising executive leaves everything behind to embark upon an incredible cross-country journey—on foot. Carrying only his backpack, Alan is determined to walk every step from Seattle to Key West. *A Step of Faith* is the fourth book in Evans's bestselling series and picks up directly after the shocking events of *The Road to Grace*. As he walks, Alan meets a number of people whose own stories help him come to terms with his grief and anger. But a life-changing event threatens to bring an end to his journey, and Alan must decide what is truly most important to him.

TOPICS & QUESTIONS FOR DISCUSSION

1. Alan writes in his diary, "Maybe, if we just accepted our deaths, we might finally start to live." How is this sentiment echoed throughout the novel? Consider some of the people Alan meets, like Dustin, who is preparing for doomsday, and Paige, who works in hospice care. How are various characters living their lives based on their acceptance or non-acceptance of death?

2. Of his mother's death when he was eight Alan says, "Some might say that she jinxed herself, but I don't think so. My mother wasn't a pessimist. I think she knew." He later reflects on a conversation he had with McKale and her request to Alan to remarry should anything happen to her. Do you think McKale may also have somehow sensed that she was going to die? Have you experienced people in your life having similar premonitions?

3. When Falene shares the news about Kyle, Alan realizes that he is actually sorry to hear it. Falene says she believes he deserved his fate. How is Alan able to feel compassion for Kyle? Do you think he is right to feel this way? Or do you agree with Falene?

4. Why is Alan blind to Falene's feelings for him until he reads her letter? Falene writes that "the depth of love is revealed in its departure." What does she mean by this? Do you think Alan's feelings about Falene would have changed without her letter and move to New York? What else influenced his feelings toward her during his journey?

5. Before Alan's surgery, Nicole and Alan's father are very nervous. "The truth was, I was the least worried of all of us," Alan says. Why is Alan able to remain so calm? Do you think he just has a feeling that he will be fine, or that he has become more at peace with the idea of his own death?

6. Why is Alan's father so against Alan returning to his walk? Given what you learn by the end of the novel, do you think his father's reasons were more complicated than you previously believed? How has their relationship changed over the course of the series?

7. When Alan spends the night at Pastor Tim's church, they discuss the existence of miracles.

"We live in an age of unbelief, but I promise you, miracles still abound," Pastor Tim says. Later that night Alan reflects on their conversation and determines that he "had prayed as sincerely as a man could for McKale's life to be spared," to no avail. Do you think his view of miracles might have changed by the end of the novel? If so, what would have caused this shift?

8. What was the significance of the scene in which Alan helps the paramedics attend to the woman who says she is having a heart attack? How might this event have affected Alan?

9. In Missouri, Alan, a longtime ad man, makes note of the many whimsical restaurant names and slogans he sees. How else does Alan display and use his "adman" background during his journey? How else does his career experience influence the way he looks at the world?

10. When Alan first encounters "Master El," the two have a conversation about how people interpret the Bible. Before you learned more about El and his group, did you agree with anything he was saying? Did any part of what he said to Alan during dinner ring true or seem plausible? Or was he completely wrong?

11. Why did Alan choose to accompany El to his compound despite his suspicions about him? Did this seem in character for Alan? El tells Alan that

those "most susceptible to mind control are precisely those who don't believe they are susceptible." Why might El think this? What did you
think about this section of the novel?

12. Do you think that if Alan's feelings for Falene
hadn't developed that he may have chosen to be
with Nicole despite his conflicted feelings about
her? Given his revelation about wanting to share
his life with someone, do you think he would
choose to settle down with someone he wasn't
fully in love with rather than spend his life alone?

13. Near the end of the novel Alan begins to believe
that "perhaps these detours *are* my journey. No
matter how much I, or the rest of humanity, wishes
otherwise, life is not lived in smooth, downhill expressways, but in the obscure, perilous trails and
back roads of life where we stumble and feel our
way through the fog of the unknown." Discuss this
passage. How does this theme resonate throughout the novel, and, if you've read them, the other
books in the series? Can you think of a time in
your life when you had a similar realization?

14. Have you been to any of the towns or sites that
Alan visits throughout the novel? What did Alan's
general impression of the southern United States
seem to be? Did his journey make you interested
in exploring any new places for yourself?

15. If you had to use only three words to describe this
book, which words would you choose?

ENHANCE YOUR BOOK CLUB

1. While Alan isn't a huge fan of Elvis's music, he thoroughly enjoys his visit to Graceland. If you're more partial to Elvis than Alan is, create a playlist of his music for your next book club. If you've been to Graceland, bring in your photos and souvenirs to share with the group. Or have an Elvis-themed dinner; there are a number of cookbooks containing recipes of his favorite dishes available from amazon.com and other bookstores.

2. Following in Alan's footsteps, plan a rambling walk with your book club (pick a day with a sunny forecast). Perhaps there are some landmarks in your town you'd like to get a closer look at. Or find an out-of-the-way grassy spot that's perfect for a picnic.

3. Share with the group a memory of a trip that you took—no matter how far away or nearby—that changed your life in some way. Were you sightseeing when a revelation hit you like a ton of bricks? Did you sample your favorite cuisine for the first time? Did you meet someone who shared valuable knowledge with you? Was it simply the most fun you've ever had?

4. Learn more about Richard Paul Evans, his books, and his charity, The Christmas Box International, at http://www.richardpaulevans.com/, http://www.facebook.com/RPEfans and https://www.thechristmasboxhouse.org/wp/.

✴ ABOUT THE AUTHOR ✴

*R*ichard Paul Evans is the #1 best-selling author of *The Christmas Box* and *Michael Vey*. Each of his twenty-two novels has been a *New York Times* bestseller. There are more than fifteen million copies of his books in print worldwide, translated into more than twenty-four languages. He is the recipient of numerous awards, including the American Mothers Book Award, the Romantic Times Best Women's Novel of the Year Award, the German Audience Gold Award for Romance, three Religion Communicators Council Wilbur Awards, the Washington Times Humanitarian of the Century Award and the Volunteers of America National Empathy Award. He lives in Salt Lake City, Utah, with his wife, Keri, and their five children. You can learn more about Richard on Facebook at www.facebook.com/RPEfans, or visit his website, www.richardpaulevans.com.

FOLLOW ALAN CHRISTOFFERSEN ON A WALK UNLIKE ANY OTHER— ONE MAN'S UNRELENTING SEARCH FOR HOPE.

The *New York Times* bestselling Walk series by

RICHARD PAUL EVANS

"Definitely a journey worth taking."
—*Booklist*

"A fast and pleasurable read with plenty of local color and enough sentiment to evoke a tear or two." —*Kirkus Reviews*

AN EXCERPT FROM

THE
FOUR DOORS

BY

✳RICHARD PAUL EVANS✳

A little more than a decade ago, I was signing books in Dayton, Ohio, when one of my readers, a schoolteacher, handed me an envelope filled with money. "My students raised this for your charity for abused children," she said. Then she asked, "Is there any way you could come thank them?"

I was in Dayton for another day, so I set a time to meet her students the following afternoon. I had expected to visit with the students, thank them for their contribution, and say a few words on the importance of reading and literacy. When I arrived at the venue, I was surprised to find buses waiting outside. Unbeknownst to me, my visit to a few students had been turned into a district-wide assembly. "You have an hour to talk to the youth," the teacher said to me.

As I frantically considered what I would say to this room full of students, the idea came to me to share with them everything I wished I knew when I was their age.

That's precisely what I did. For the next hour I spoke from the heart, and the teens sat in complete silence. About halfway through my talk, I noticed that some of the youth were crying. When I finished, the students stood to applaud, then lined up to meet me. Some of them wanted to share with me their own stories and struggles. Some of them just asked to be hugged.

That afternoon was the beginning of a journey for me, one that has taken me all around the world, sharing this message with hundreds of thousands of people from remarkably diverse groups ranging from the American Mothers, Inc., Harvard MBA graduates, and the Million Dollar Round Table (a global association of the world's top insurance agents and financial service professionals) to recovering drug addicts and convicted felons. And just like the first time I shared these principles, in each of those subsequent presentations I have also witnessed a powerful reaction. And, after every presentation, audience members have asked for a written copy of my talk so that they too could share these principles with those they care about. This book is the result of those requests.

Initially, my talk didn't have a name and I just referred to it as "the talk." It was more than five years after that first presentation before I began calling my talk "The Four Doors." I liked the metaphor of the door for two reasons. First, because passing through a door requires knowledge, intent, and action. We can't pass through a door we can't find and we can't pass through a door without moving ourselves.

Second, once we've crossed a door's threshold, we are not in the same place as we were before. These characteristics are true for each of the doors, or principles, in this book.

I believe that the greatest thing that all humanity has in common is the desire to make their lives matter. In the last two decades, I have met thousands of people and heard many of their stories. Far too many are living what Thoreau termed "lives of quiet desperation." They live far below their own potential for joy, accomplishment, and power, caged in the prisons of their own unknowing. To some degree, this describes all of us.

The Four Doors is about how to live life joyfully, with freedom, power, and purpose. I have witnessed the powerful effect each of these doors carries—in both my own life and the lives of those with whom I have shared this message. If you are willing to follow even just one of these principles, you will find immediate, positive change in your life. If you choose to live them all, you will soon be in a very different place than you are now. The choice is yours. And, as you will soon learn, the Four Doors are entirely about choice.